ONE
PARTICULAR
HARBOUR

A JAKE SULLIVAN NOVEL

THE JAKE SULLIVAN SERIES

Come Monday

Trying to Reason with Hurricane Season

Havana Daydreamin'

A Pirate Looks at Forty

One Particular Harbour

ALSO AVAILABLE:

Trilogy

COMING SOON:

Son of a Son of a Sailor

ONE PARTICULAR HARBOUR

A JAKE SULLIVAN NOVEL

CHIP BELL

"Most mysterious calling harbour
So far but yet so near."

- "One Particular Harbour" by Jimmy Buffett

To Linda, for always allowing me my schemes and dreams.

ACKNOWLEDGEMENT

To Eve, who somehow always manages to get it done.

ATLANTIC   OCEAN

Anegada

⊙ The Settlement

BRITISH
VIRGIN ISLANDS

Jost Van
Dyke

Great
Harbour

Guana I.

Great
Camanoe

Beef I.

Tortola

Virgin Gorda

ROAD
TOWN

Spanish
Town

Great
Thatch I.

West End

St. John

Salt I.

Ginger I.

Norman I.

Copper I.

Peter I.

Mona Lollik I.

CHARLOTTE
AMALIE

St. John

St. Thomas

Red Hook

Water I.

Cruz Bay

Virgin Islands
National Park

UNITED STATES
VIRGIN ISLANDS

CARIBBEAN   SEA

Buck I.

St. Croix

Christiansted

Frederiksted

PROLOGUE

(TWO MONTHS PREVIOUS)

ST. CROIX

U.S. V.I.

CHAPTER 1

In the office of Adolphus Hamilton, CEO and Chairman of the Board of Hamilton Industries, a distant relative of Alexander Hamilton, his family having migrated to the island of St. Croix from the island of Nevis, he lit a hand-rolled Cuban cigar as he looked out the windows of the corporate offices located on Company Street in Christiansted.

Looking past the Old Dutch West India Company warehouse and D. Hamilton Jackson Park, onward to Gallows Bay, the fit sixty-four year old, resplendent in a perfectly tailored navy blue suit, and blue and red striped tie, smiled at his reflection in the glass.

On the desk lay open an old copy of the Virgin Island Daily News, and on the computer screen the latest posting from the St. Croix Source, the local on-line newspaper.

In his other hand, he held a glass of specially distilled Cruzan Rum, still made at the centuries old distillery on West Airport Road, and smiled as he took a sip, realizing that fate was about to provide him with what he had always wanted: fame . . . power . . . fortune . . . and revenge.

He sat down and once again studied the yellowed newspaper photo. He gazed intently at the fuzzy photograph of a tall, dark-haired man smiling as he held out his hand to receive an award presented to him at the famous Columbia Restaurant by the Ybor

City Chamber of Commerce for his efforts in a series of prosecutions that decimated one of the most feared street gangs in the area.

He sat back, his eyes taking in the room, and he reached for the phone on the desk, stopping to look at the far wall where a portrait of a young, beautiful, dark-haired woman gazed back at him. Imagining his coming triumph, he raised his glass toward the portrait and toasted . . . "And for you, too, young lady." After taking another drink, he set the glass on the desk and pressed a button on the phone, his gaze shifting toward the opposite wall of windows looking South over the island, and once again he smiled at the far distant glow along the western edge of Cane Garden Bay rising over Jerusalem and Fig Tree Hill, emanating from the lights of the now-abandoned oil refinery at Krause Lagoone.

A voice came from the speaker on the phone. "Yes sir, what is it?"

Looking at the computer screen announcing that the Annual Bench-Bar Conference of the Third Circuit Court of Appeals was to be held at Caneel Bay in the coming weeks and the list of speakers who would be presenting at the Conference, smiling, he spoke, "Mr. Dalton, it is time to set our operation into motion. Fate has been kind to us and I have devised a plan that will bring great success to me . . . economically, politically, and most of all, personally. Please come at once."

As was the habit of a man in his position, he never waited for a reply. Pressing another button on the phone to disconnect, he sat back in the chair, his visage in shadows from the soft light of the desk lamp, clearly that of one who believed his time had come.

MIAMI, FLORIDA

U.S.A.

CHAPTER 2

Eva had just finished putting away the last of the files Mike Lang had plopped on her desk that afternoon. Looking at the clock and seeing that it was almost 5:30, she decided it was time to call it a day, straightened her desk, and grabbed her purse. Taking out her cell phone, she checked to see if she had any messages before walking into the office of her boss, Jake Sullivan, Chief Federal Prosecutor of the Miami Office of the Justice Department. Knowing how much he hated paperwork, she had to laugh as she saw Mike Lang, Jake's chief investigator and best friend, hunched over a stack of papers, muttering to himself as he filled out forms on the latest RICO case in which he and Jake had been involved.

"Smile!" chirped Eva, as she pointed the camera at Mike, who lifted his head, staring at her, with anything but a smile. The click and quick flash indicated her cell phone had done the job and she looked at the screen. "Great picture. I'm sending this to Jake right now while he's on the plane. I'm sure he'll be happy to see how you're taking care of the office while he's gone, especially using his desk."

"You know," said Mike, "I know I'm only filling out these forms for Jake to take a look at when he gets back, but I don't know how he stands all this paperwork without going crazy."

"All part of the job, hon," said Eva. "I'm calling it a day and heading home."

Mike spoke to her back as she headed out the door. "You know, he could have taken me with him."

Eva turned. "Yes, but I'm so glad he didn't."

"Like having me around that much?" said Mike, smiling broadly.

"Oh sure, I like having you here hon! If it wasn't for you, who do you think would be doing all that preliminary paperwork?" With that, Eva returned his smile, turned and was gone.

It was Mike's turn to look at the clock, which was now approaching 5:45.

"He should be landing soon," thought Mike, turning back to the pile in front of him, and repeating under his breath, "I still can't believe he didn't take me with him."

ST. THOMAS

U.S. V.I.

CHAPTER 3

The passenger in seat 14C yawned and stretched his legs as the airplane descended to the Cyril E. King Airport on the island of St. Thomas, just outside Charlotte Amalie, the capital of the U.S. Virgin Islands. He stretched his lean 6'2" frame, ran his hand through his dark, reddish-brown hair, slightly turning gray at the temples, and looked out the window with green piercing eyes, thinking to himself that if he was not going to the conference in the Virgin Islands he would be back in Miami doing paperwork on a Wednesday at the end of March. The stewardess, Lorie, who had been very attentive during the almost 3-hour flight from Miami, came by and asked if she could get him another Diet Coke. Smiling back, he told her that he was fine, just as the signal sounded for everyone to take their seats and buckle up for the landing.

"Not a bad trip," said Jake, directing his comments to Arlen Jacobsen, a prominent Philadelphia trial lawyer with whom Jake had kept up a running conversation during the flight.

"I've certainly had worse," said Jacobsen. "Ready for your time in paradise?"

Jake undid his seatbelt, rose, and took his bag and briefcase out of the overhead compartment. He couldn't help but laugh to himself as he replied, "It never ceases to amaze me how judges and lawyers make sure that their annual conferences are held at some of the best resort venues in the world. Of course, nobody could fault the Third Circuit since it hears the appeals of the U.S. Territorial Court of the Virgin Islands."

"Yeah," said Jacobsen, "funny how this particular spot became assigned to the Third Circuit in 1948. Think it's a coincidence that the Third Circuit is comprised of the Middle Atlantic states with all those New York and Pennsylvania lawyers?"

Jake laughed again as Jacobsen also rose and took out his materials from the overhead.

"You're not trying to tell me that there was some type of collusion in play, are you?"

Looking back over his shoulder, Jacobsen smiled. "Jake, all I can tell you is that the term 'Philadelphia Lawyer' came into being for a reason."

They shook hands before departing the aircraft.

"A pleasure, Jake. Watch your step. Try not to piss off Alito too much."

Jake returned the handshake and smiled back. "I'll do what I can, but I have a feeling that's already a done deal."

Each United States Supreme Court Justice was assigned a Circuit Court, and presently Justice Samuel Alito held that position for the Third Circuit and would be speaking at the conference on Friday night. Jake, however, due to the celebrity status he had attained from the notoriety garnered from the Benjamin Matthews, Meyer Lansky, and Mem events, was the keynote speaker, giving the address on Saturday night. Jacobsen had spent the entire flight goading Jake about how angry Alito was going to be that it wasn't him.

Jake called out to Jacobsen as he moved ahead, "I guess I'll just have to use my charm on him."

Jacobsen came to a halt and turned before exiting the door of the plane. "That's the best you got?" He shook his head, smiling, and was gone.

Just as Jake was following him out the door, shaking his head, too, his phone beeped. Taking it out, he saw that he had received a text and opened it. Knowing Eva and Mike as well as he did, he couldn't help but laugh at the picture of Mike sitting at his desk with all that paperwork in front of him, and he could almost hear him complaining to Eva about not going on the trip.

"Sorry Mike," he thought to himself, "but I think I can give a speech without getting into any trouble."

CHAPTER 4

Jake had determined not to take the shuttle from the airport directly to the Caneel Bay Resort and bypassed the Caneel Bay Reception Center and headed for the taxi stand, where he hailed a cab. Jake believed it was proper for him, as a representative of the United States Government, to check-in with his counterpart, Arthur Braxton, the U.S. Attorney for the District of the Virgin Islands, and told the cab driver to take him to the Federal Building and U.S. Courthouse at 5500 Veterans Drive, even though this meant that he would miss the last Charlotte Amalie-Cruz Bay Ferry leaving Kings Wharf and he would have to go to Red Hook to catch another ferry to the island of St. John.

They had not gone far when Jake noticed the cab driver was staring in the rearview mirror. Jake looked at him quizzically.

"I'm sorry," said the cabbie. "I didn't mean to stare, but you're Jake Sullivan, right?"

Jake smiled to himself and with a slight shake of his head said, "I am."

"My name's Frank . . . Frank Dempsey. It's a pleasure to meet you. I've read a lot about you."

"Yea, well don't believe everything you read," said Jake.

The cabbie laughed. "Don't be modest, Mr. Sullivan. You've done some pretty good things."

Jake noticed the accent. "You're not from here, are you, Mr. Dempsey?"

"No, I'm not, and call me Frank. Actually, I'm from the Bronx."

"And?" questioned Jake.

"Same old story. I actually managed a hedge fund for a while on Wall Street until 2008 when the shit hit the fan. Lost everything, my wife divorced me, kids had to quit their private schools, they hate me, and finally . . . the SEC was sniffing around . . . so I just took off. Ended up here. Doing a little of this . . . a little of that. And right now you're a part of the 'little of this."

Jake looked out the side window and noticed some of the brightly colored walls of buildings that were pasted with signs, all proclaiming something or other for the PIVI.

"What's the PIVI?" Jake asked the cabbie.

"You want the long version or the short version?"

"Whatever we have enough time for," said Jake.

"PIVI stands for the Party for an Independent Virgin Islands," said the cabbie. "They want independence from the United States and an end to territorial rule, and they're run by some Marxist whacko named Andre Bollinger."

"I don't think I've ever heard of him," said Jake.

"Not a lot of the people outside of the islands have, although your pal the President takes notice of him. Bollinger's a rabble-rouser. He's always somewhere giving a speech on why the islands should be a free and independent country, how capitalism is no good, and he uses HOVIC to prove his point."

"HOVIC?" Jake asked quizzically.

"Yea, Hess Oil formed a corporation down here called Hess Oil Virgin Islands Corporation . . . HOVIC for short . . . and opened the largest oil refinery in the Western Hemisphere at Krause Lagoone on the western edge of Cane Garden Bay on St. Croix in 1966. By 1974, it was one of the largest producers of oil in the world. Four years later, in 1978, Hess somehow decided to align with Petroleos de Venezuela S.A., the state-owned oil company in Venezuela. Now the people in Washington were getting a little antsy because they've already heard of Chavez and know he's a socialist, and they're worried about the control of that much oil in the wrong hands. In the meantime, the new company, which is now called Hovensa, became the largest employer on the island, with about 2,000 jobs.

Well, as everybody says, it's a global marketplace right? So sure enough, oil production began to spike everywhere else around the planet. Hovensa would have had to re-tool the whole plant to increase capacity ... price per barrel was going down due to the glut on the market ... and in February 2012 Hovensa decided to shut down. It ceased operations at the plant, made it a storage terminal only since they had hit about $1.3 billion in losses over the previous three years. Now what Bollinger did was take that closing and he ran with it. To him it was a symbol of the failure of United States capitalism, and he shouted that from the rooftops, giving political clout to the PIVI.

Allegedly, Bollinger had been an ally of LaBeet back in the 1980s."

"Wait a minute," said Jake, "that name's familiar."

"It should be," said the cabbie. Looking back in the mirror, he said, "Given your age, you were probably just finishing college when the Fountain Valley Massacre occurred on what is known today as the Carambola Golf Course on St. Croix, when Ishmael Ali LaBeet and four associates massacred eight people. After hiding out in the islands until 1984, LaBeet skyjacked a plane and forced the pilot to take him to Cuba. Bollinger was an alleged part of that.

Bollinger's not stupid, even though he's a devout Marxist. He sensed his popularity growing, realized what he needed was political clout ... so he renounced terrorism, made the PIVI a purely political party, played on the joblessness that came from the closing of the refinery, and promised a new day for a free and independent Virgin Islands. And if it wasn't for your President Fletcher, he might well have been the new Territorial Governor."

"You're kidding me," said Jake.

"Nope. If it hadn't been a three-way race, he might have had enough votes to win it all . . . that and the fact that the United States government poured a ton of money into the campaign of one James R. Sterling, who renounced everything Bollinger stood for. When those two were in the race, it was neck-and-neck, but then our State Prosecutor, Philip Donaldson, got into the act and declared himself a candidate . . . came out of the blue with a ton of money behind him. Rumors were the money was from some corporate group who wanted to restart the refinery. See, Bollinger was dead-set against it because that was his trump card. He wanted to make the place green again . . . a wildlife sanctuary. He still goes on and on about removing the stain of failed capitalism on the island and creating green jobs for the people. It's all crap, but it sells. Sterling took the middle road and said the factory could be turned into some other type of plant for green energy, taking on the position of President, which I'm sure he was told to do. But Donaldson entered the race. He made no bones about it. He wanted to reopen the refinery as a refinery . . . start production all over again . . . bring back all the jobs that were lost. So all three were in a tight race and when election day came, the weight of the White House and the money from the mainland went out, and Sterling is now our Territorial Governor. But the other two factions . . . that conglomerate that wants the refinery back and the PIVI . . . came close . . . and they both know it. So next election season, we're in for a battle."

"Who do you think will win?" asked Jake.

"No telling," said Dempsey. "Look, you've got a situation where there's a long history of colonial rule. The thought of independence is always floating out there, but the economic ties with the United States have been more helpful than harmful to these islands, and while the general population may like to yell and scream, those in positions of power know it. They're scared to death of the PIVI, and I think they'll probably do anything and everything to make sure Bollinger is not the next Territorial Governor. Sorry to talk your ear off, Mr. Sullivan, but we're here," said Dempsey as he pulled the cab to a stop.

"Hey, no problem. I appreciate the history lesson. I asked the question, so thanks for the answer. Listen, would you mind coming around again in an hour to drive me to Red Hook so I can catch the ferry over to St. John?"

Dempsey looked at his watch. "It'd be a pleasure, Mr. Sullivan. I'll be right here."

"Thanks Frank, I appreciate it," as he handed Dempsey payment.

"No thanks, Mr. Sullivan . . . on the house. I don't get that many celebrities, and there are very few people that let me talk that much."

Jake laughed and dropped the bills down in Dempsey's lap. "First of all, I'm not a celebrity, and second of all, I enjoyed the conversation. I'll see you in an hour."

"Thanks Mr. Sullivan," Dempsey offered to Jake's back as he was walking away.

Without turning, Jake raised his hand and waved and headed into the Federal Building.

After going through the metal detector and scanners and providing his credentials to the guard, he made his way into Room 260, the U.S. Attorney's Office, and was greeted warmly by Arthur Braxton.

Braxton was a big man with a face the color of dark mahogany. He had been born here in St. Croix and had made his way out

– got an education and got a job with the Justice Department after several less than stellar years in private practice. There had been rumors over the years that he was unhappy, that he felt he had been passed over because of his race and age, and his inability to work with the "good ole boys", but Jake had always gotten along with the older man.

"Jake, good to see you! What's it been? Three years or better?"

"More like four or five, Arthur," said Jake, who had been to many training sessions and conferences with Arthur in their early years in the Justice Department.

"So tell me," said Jake, "what's it like having such a plum job in paradise?"

"Jake, I wish I could tell you I sat here with my feet propped on my desk, sipping a drink with an umbrella in it until it was time to go to the beach, but lately, this place has been anything but paradise. PIVI's constant rants against the United States and its calls for independence have made me more a diplomat than a lawyer, which isn't very good 'cause I'm not the diplomatic type."

"Is it really that bad, Arthur?" asked Jake.

"When you take a combination of the old hard feelings against colonial rule and add to them the promise of jobs on an island with one of the highest unemployment rates in the world, you have a lethal combination . . . and Bollinger's good at it. He paints himself as the savior of the people of the islands and that idea is starting to gain traction. The word we get is he is pushing for a referendum for early next year to vote on independence. If that referendum passes, given the current balance of power in Congress, it's going to cause some serious problems for the President. But enough of that," said Braxton, "let me just sit here and bask in the aura of the celebrity that is Jake Sullivan."

"Cut the crap, Arthur," said Jake. "You know me better than that. Those situations just sort of found me. I didn't go looking for them."

"I'm sure that's true, Jake," said Braxton, "but you gotta admit, you pulled off some great jobs the last couple of years. You probably saved Fletcher's job, might have saved the country, cemented the treaty with Cuba, and found all that money. And then there was the Israeli matter. Not bad for a Miami lawyer. And now you get top billing over Alito . . . what more could you ask for?"

"Like I asked for it," said Jake with a smile. "I should be sitting on the beach with one of those drinks you mentioned actually having a vacation, rather than getting the cold shoulder from Justice Alito when I'm introduced to him."

"Yeah, I'm sure he's not going to be too happy taking a back seat."

"I wouldn't think so," said Jake. "And I'm sure I'm about to find out."

Just then, there was a knock in the doorway and Braxton stood up.

"Jake, I want you to meet Bill Adams, Special Agent in charge of our local FBI. I believe Bill is an old buddy of your cohort in arms, Mike Lang."

"Good to meet you, Mr. Sullivan," said Bill, extending his hand.

"Please, call me Jake."

"All right Jake, how's my old buddy Mike Lang doing?"

"Well, right now he's sitting in an office in Miami, or maybe by now he's left, having gone through a day of paperwork, which he hates, and cursing me for not bringing him along on this trip."

Adams laughed. "That sounds like Mike, especially the part about hating paperwork. Through all our days at the academy and the period of time I worked with him on the Drug Task Force, he was one of the best field agents I ever knew, but God did he hate the paperwork that followed."

"Look . . . between you and me, and make sure this doesn't get back to Mike, I never would have survived those adventures Art and I just talked about without him. And if anybody ever needs someone to back them up, there's no question that Mike's the guy to go to."

Bill chuckled to himself and looked at Jake. "You sure you don't want me to tell him that, huh?"

"You know Mike," said Jake, "would you tell him if you were me?"

"Not a chance," said Bill. "Listen, it was good to meet you, but I have to get back to work. For some funny reason, the criminals still operate here in paradise. We've got an arms smuggling deal going on right now."

"It must be the tropics," said Jake. "Same thing is going on in Miami all the time."

"I hear you," said Bill. "Take care of yourself, and hopefully I'll get the chance to talk to you later."

"Good meeting you, too," said Jake.

And with that, Adams was out the door.

"Listen, Art, I just wanted to make sure I stopped in to see you while I was still on the island. I'm going to go catch the ferry from Red Hook to Cruz Bay and get settled in. I've got a little work to do on my speech."

"No problem, Jake. Listen, don't worry about a cab, I'll have one of the drivers here take you over."

"That's not necessary, Art. I have a friend picking me up. I'll talk to you later. We have a lot of catching up to do . . . all those old times."

"Absolutely," said Braxton, "make sure you check in with me before you leave paradise."

"Will do," said Jake. And with that, he was gone.

Braxton sat down at his desk, picked up his reading glasses, and started working on the file from which Jake had interrupted him. Looking at his watch, he realized he had calls to make. Reaching for the phone, he thought to himself, "I'm with you, Mr. Lang. The paperwork can wait."

CHAPTER 5

True to his word, Frank Dempsey was sitting with his taxi idling when Jake exited the Federal Building.

Their political conversation having come to an end, the ride consisted only of small chit-chat, and Jake mainly sat back and enjoyed the ride.

It was approximately 8:00 P.M., and barely enough daylight to allow him to make out the view along Route 32, with the lights from the ships beyond Compass Point starting to come on. They traveled on Turpentine Run to Red Hook Road, hugging the southern coast along Benner Bay until they arrived at Red Hook and the terminal for the Red Hook-Cruz Bay Ferry.

After he and Dempsey made their goodbyes, Jake boarded the ferry and found a seat in the open air and was able to sit back and stretch out, suddenly becoming somewhat tired after the day's activities. He started to doze just as the ferry crossed Pillsbury Sound and the last thing he remembered was the lights of Gallows Point in the distance, marking the opening into Cruz Bay and the island of St. John.

ST. JOHN

U.S. V.I.

CHAPTER 6

A slowing of the ferry engines woke Jake and he realized they had arrived in Cruz Bay. Checking on his things, he noticed in the side pocket of his bag the pamphlet the conference attendees all had all been given concerning Caneel Bay.

Now run by the Leading Hotels of the World, Ltd., the resort was originally created by Laurance Rockefeller and was one of the original hotels in the Rock Resort Hotel chain. Taking its name from the old Dutch word for cinnamon, Caneel Bay is nestled in the Virgin Islands National Park, property donated by Rockefeller to the United States government after he had arranged to buy up most of the island of St. John. The resort and its beaches have always been considered one of the most beautiful in the world.

Exiting the ferry after it docked, Jake found the Jeep that was waiting to take him and other guests to the Caneel Bay Resort. They took the North Shore Road past Solomon Beach and Honeymoon Bay, and entered the resort past the sugar mill ruins, drove past the coffee shop, the gelateris and gift shop, and parked near the Sunset Terrace. Jake exited and entered the lobby to check in.

He was assigned Suite 14, just off the Beach Terrace, with a breathtaking view of Caneel Bay.

After providing the necessary documentation, credit card, and identification, he received his conference packet and was met by a concierge, who walked him the short distance to his suite.

After tipping the concierge, Jake flopped down on the large double bed, his body waging an internal battle of sleep versus hunger. Sleep won out, and still fully dressed, he was soon sound asleep.

The ringing at first was low and Jake thought it was part of a dream. It slowly grew louder, and finally he realized the phone on the bed stand was ringing. Looking at his watch, he realized it was a little after 11:00 o'clock and that he had fallen asleep as soon as he had laid down.

Reaching for the phone, he answered, "Hello? . . . Hello?" but there was no one there. "Great," thought Jake. He laid back down and must have dozed off again, but not in the deep sleep he was in before.

There was a sound, and it woke him – not loud, just something out of place – and he rose to a sitting position and tried to clear his eyes as he looked around the room. Again looking at his watch, he decided. "I might as well call it a night," he said as he headed toward for the door to check the security lock and the deadbolt. It was then that he noticed what appeared to be a manila envelope that someone had slid under his door.

Picking up the envelope and noticing there were no markings on it, he went back to the bed and sat down. Breaking the seal and opening the clasp, he slid out a blank piece of paper, which had a handwritten note:

"Meet me at the beach bar and grill. I have information on the entire group who were working with Matthews. Midnight."

"You've got to be kidding," thought Jake. "Matthews? Now? Here?"

Benjamin Matthews, the former Attorney General. The man who had gained control of the international drug trade, who almost gained complete control of the Mexican drug cartels and was using the drug money for what amounted to a coup to become President of the United States, who had kidnapped Jake's family, who had tried to have him killed, who had killed the woman Mike loved, Paula Cortez, and whom Mike ultimately killed in Havana.

"He still seems to haunt me," thought Jake.

He gave serious thought to ripping up the note, throwing it away, and climbing under the covers and pretending he never heard of Benjamin Matthews, but he knew that he couldn't. Matthews had a vast conspiracy in place, and there were rumors now and again that Matthews' operatives were still in place in government and elsewhere, just waiting for a leader to take charge again and resurrect the entire organization. If there was any truth to that note, it was information Jake had to have.

Sighing deeply and shaking his head, and looking at his watch once again to make sure he had time, he headed for the bathroom to take a quick shower, wanting to make sure he had a clear head and that he was sharp for the meeting that was about to come. After the shower, he quickly tore off the towel he was wearing as he headed for his bag and put on a colorful island shirt, a pair of shorts, and his Sanuks.

As he exited the door, he couldn't help but feel that something had changed. He sensed paradise turning darker, but he wasn't sure why. Most of all, he wondered if he had made a mistake. He wondered if he should have brought Mike.

CHAPTER 7

The corporate jet of Hamilton Industries had landed in Miami early that morning, and Mr. Dalton wasted no time in proceeding to the office building housing the U.S. Attorney's Office at 99 Northeast 4th Street, having stashed the various outfits and documents he might need in a van, which, as had been arranged, was waiting for him at the airport parking lot.

When he first entered the building, he was wearing a $2,000.00 summer suit bearing the name tag of one of Miami's most prestigious law firms, identifying him as one Lawrence Talbot, Attorney at Law. The young female security guard seemed duly impressed by the handsome, tanned attorney, and he was passed through and sent on his way without incident, free to roam the halls of the building, which he did for several hours, obtaining what he needed to know, and exiting the building the same way he had come in.

Moving the van, he found a parking spot on Biscayne Boulevard where he had a vantage point of the entrance to the office building. He killed time by strolling along the Boulevard and in Bay Front Park.

Having memorized by heart the complete dossier supplied to him by his employer, including photographs of the individuals in play and knowing exactly what his employer's plan entailed, he did not have to wait long until he recognized Jake Sullivan leaving the building parking lot around 1:00 P.M. in his BMW Z4, heading for the airport for his 3:00 o'clock flight to St. Thomas.

Similarly, he recognized Eva, Sullivan's secretary, when she left the office building at approximately 5:30 P.M., and Mike Lang, the investigator, when he left a half hour or so later.

The information he had been given indicated that the cleaning crews began to arrive at approximately 6:00 P.M. He had already changed into a gun-metal gray work uniform in the van and had clipped the name tag he had been provided onto his shirt pocket. He watched the doors and waited until two or three similarly attired men had entered, then exited the van and headed toward the building. His naturally sandy hair was now covered with a dark wig, his upper lip sported a dark mustache, and what appeared to be thick corrective lenses sat on the bridge of his nose. He walked with a slight shuffle and his Welsh-Slavic tinged accent was now clearly replaced with one from the American South, slightly slurred and hard to understand.

As he approached the entry point, he noticed that the guard on duty's name was Tully. Lowering his head in deference, he nodded.

"Evening Mr. Tully."

The guard looked at him carefully, staring at his name tag. "Reardon . . . I don't recognize you, Reardon."

Still looking down, Mr. Reardon said, "I'm just a sub Mr. Tully. I only come in when someone else is sick or calls off. That's why I'm a little late. I just got a call to come in. I think this is only the third or fourth time I've been in this building. Sure is big . . . nice though," he said looking around, seemingly in awe, then looking down quickly at his feet again.

Tully stared, not quite sure, and Reardon thought to himself, "I need to close this quickly."

Stepping forward with a line he had been practicing, he said, "Would it be all right if I would get to work now, Mr. Tully? I'm only here for an hour and I want to work real fast, but do everything real good now, but real fast 'cause I want to get home for Wheel of Fortune. Momma and I really like that program, so I want to get back so we can see it. Do you watch that, Mr. Tully?"

Tully just shook his head. "All right Reardon, go ahead, go through. Go ahead and get to work. I don't want you to miss your program."

"Thanks Mr. Tully, thank you, sir."

Satisfied that the guard would not forget Mr. Reardon and be able to describe him to a "T" when the time came, the janitor smiled and made his way to the elevators, taking one to the offices of the Justice Department. He worked his way through the offices, moving the cart he had taken from its prearranged place, emptying waste baskets and dusting as would be expected of him. He only came in contact with one other person the whole time he was in the offices, and that was one of the night guards patrolling the floor. Reardon was busy mopping an area of tiled floor when the guard opened the door and looked in. Seeing Reardon's cart and him fast at work, the guard just nodded, and Reardon nodded in reply. Without a word, the guard closed the door and was on his way, and Reardon smiled at how easy this job had been so far.

When he got to the office of the Chief Prosecuting Attorney, he moved around behind the desk, again making a show of dusting and straightening, but then he stopped, alert for any noise that was out of place, any movement in the hallways or in the office. Hearing none, he quickly reached up on the credenza behind the desk and removed the item he had been sent to retrieve. He slipped it into a pouch that had been specially made for it and sewn into the inside of the pants he was wearing. From a similar pouch on one of his cargo-style pockets, he took out a disc and quickly sat down at the computer and uploaded the data. Checking his work and making sure the information was where it should be, he rose and moved the desk chair back into place. Satisfied that he had accomplished his mission, he then moved out into the hallway and continued cleaning other offices.

Placing the cart back where he had found it, he took the elevator down to the lobby and hurriedly walked past his good friend Tully, waving as he did.

"Told you I was gonna hustle tonight, Mr. Tully. Everything is done. You can go up and check those offices. They're clean as a whistle."

Tully looked at his watch and half laughed, "Reardon, I'm sure if they're not, you'll hear about it. Go enjoy your program," as he waved Reardon out the door.

Exiting the building, Dalton headed back to his van and removed his disguise, changing back into floral shirt, shorts, and flip-flops. Looking at his watch, he had plenty of time to make the 7:30 rendezvous he had previously arranged to take care of one last detail.

Alfredo Ramirez, a postal employee in Miami's Central Post Office, had determined the location and Dalton was happy he was able to find a parking lot near Hoi Como Ayer, a popular dance club in Little Havana.

As was his habit, Dalton checked every aspect of the bar as he entered, looking for exit routes, suspicious types, and anything that might prove a detriment or an aid in certain situations. He had come early solely for that purpose and sat down at the bar to wait for Mr. Ramirez.

It was still not too crowded, the late night dance patrons not having yet arrived, when Dalton saw Ramirez entering, carrying a plastic bag. He recognized him immediately from their prior encounter. Ramirez saw him at the bar and moved over and took a seat that Dalton had saved.

"How are you, Alfredo?" said a smiling Dalton, patting him on the back.

Ramirez was sweating profusely, and Dalton noticed his hand shake was weak and damp.

"I took the chance you still drank Mojitos," said Dalton as he waved to the bartender, who brought over a tall, chilled glass topped with a sprig of fresh mint.

Ramirez's hand shook as he reached for the glass and took a long drink.

"You have my money?" he whispered.

"Of course Alfredo, of course. We had a deal. I presume everything went smoothly?"

Ramirez shook his head anxiously. "It did, it did. I found a piece of metal the exact weight that you had given me, put on the address label and return address that you had provided, and sent it out on the day you requested." Handing him the small slip, he said, "Here is the tracking information, but the package should already be there. The other box for mailing back to Miami is here in this bag."

"Excellent Alfredo! Excellent! I'm sure it is." Dalton looked around. "It's getting a little too crowded in here to conduct our business, Alfredo. Let's go to the parking lot. I have your package in the trunk." Dalton sensed a change in Ramirez, his look changing to one of suspicion tinged with fear.

"Why can't we conclude our business right here, in the light, with all these people?"

Moving closer, Dalton whispered in his ear, "Alfredo, this is not the type of business I like to conduct in front of so many witnesses. You know whose name you put on those packages. We must keep this a very private matter." Slapping him on the back, he continued, "Come on Alfredo. Let's get done and you can come back in and buy the bar a round, if you so choose."

The initial fear having passed, Ramirez shook his head and followed Dalton out the door to the parking lot, moving to the van where Dalton began to unlock the back door. Ramirez stopped and looked at him.

"Wait a minute, you told me you had my money in the trunk."

Dalton looked at Ramirez and sighed, "So I did Alfredo, so I did." Walking toward him, holding out his hands as if he was surrendering, "A mistake on my part." Shaking his head slightly, he went on, "Something I usually don't make." Moving with the speed that came from years of training, he lunged at Alfredo and spun him around, holding his forearm under his chin, dragging him into the shadows between two parked vehicles, slowing cutting off the airflow until Ramirez went unconscious.

Searching through his pockets, he found a set of car keys and moved out into the open, ensuring that there were no witnesses, and began pressing the automatic entry button as he scanned the parking lot with the keys until a set of lights and a beep came from a tan Toyota parked several cars away. Picking up the fallen bag, he picked up Ramirez and, putting one arm around his neck and over his shoulders, he dragged him through the parking lot, loudly talking and laughing to him about what a time they had and how much Ramirez had to drink. They passed a young couple who were about to enter the bar from the parking lot and Dalton, now in fluent Spanish, loudly congratulated the couple on their looks, hoping that they would remember the drunk Ramirez and his friend.

Opening the Toyota's front driver door, Dalton positioned Ramirez behind the steering wheel, and when he was satisfied, bent down and took off a shoe and sock. Taking a syringe out of his pocket, he took off the cap and injected the contents between the little and next toe of Ramirez's foot, a spot that normally would not be checked since the serum he had injected would give every indication that Ramirez had suffered a heart attack after a heavy night of drinking.

Dalton knelt down and waited and saw the spasms begin in Ramirez's chest and quickly end. He checked for a pulse, and when he found none, once again looked at the scene, put back on the sock and shoe, wiped off anything he may have touched, put the keys on the floor where they would have fallen out of Ramirez's right hand, shut the door, took the bag with the mailing box with him, and quickly made his way back to the van, exited the parking lot, and headed for the airport, where the corporate jet was waiting and would have him in St. Thomas in less than two and one-half hours.

ST. THOMAS
ST. JOHN
U.S. V.I.

CHAPTER 8

The plane had made good headway and actually touched down at Cyril E. King Airport in a little less than two hours. A company car was waiting for him on the tarmac, as had been arranged, and quickly took him to the docks in Charlotte Amalie, where he boarded a motor boat, which immediately headed for the island of St. John.

The boat made its way out of St. Thomas Harbor and along the southeastern portion of the island, passed between Water Point and Great St. James Island, across the Pillsbury Sound, turned slightly north, and made its way past Gallows Point and into Cruz Bay.

Dalton, still dressed in his floral shirt, shorts, and flip-flops, the packages from Miami secured in a small duffle bag he was carrying, moved swiftly to the car that had been waiting for him next to the launch's mooring spot. There were two men standing outside the car. Upon seeing Dalton, one quickly headed to take the driver's position and started the engine, and the other opened the door for Dalton to enter the back seat behind the driver, closed it, and quickly got in the front passenger's seat. They then headed for the Caneel Bay Resort as had been arranged, their vehicle approaching a small cutoff to the right of North Shore Road when a set of lights quickly flashed. Pulling over, Dalton got out, having taken the package out of his duffle bag, and moved toward the vehicle, where a rear window was going down. Looking in, he handed over the package.

"You have him, I presume?" said Dalton.

"Everything is taken care of," came the reply.

"Then I'll see you on the beach shortly. Remember . . . no mistakes."

"As I said, Mr. Dalton, everything is taken care of."

Dalton watched the figure in the car set down the package and continued looking.

"What are you staring at?" came the voice.

Dalton just smirked. "Nothing. Funny though . . . old habits never die," and he turned and quickly returned to his own vehicle, which then continued on its way to the Caneel Bay Resort.

Having exited the vehicle and entered the reception area, Dalton moved off to the side to make sure he was not observed and quickly hit a preset number. Moving quickly, he approached the desk, speaking softly into the phone so as not to be overheard. "Mr. Jake Sullivan, please," and arrived at the desk, smiling broadly and in time to see the desk clerk punch in Suite 14. Holding the phone against his thigh to muffle the sound, he heard Jake Sullivan respond to the call.

"What a beautiful night!" he exclaimed as the desk clerk named Samuel looked up from his computer screen and half-heartedly smiled back.

Picking a number at random, Vaughan asked, "Any messages for Suite 23?" having shut off the cell phone now that the call had gone through and he had gained the knowledge he needed without attracting attention. When the clerk replied there was none, Vaughan turned and waved back, "It's off to bed for me then. Goodnight."

A halfhearted, "Good night," followed Vaughan as he made his way toward the door that led to the bank of suites that included Suite 23.

Making sure he was out of sight of the front desk, Vaughan veered off the corridor and made his way back, skirting the wall, glancing around until he was sure that the desk clerk was once again buried in his computer screen, and skirted past the front desk to a side door, which Vaughan had already studied and knew led to the mail room.

Taking out a small packet of tools, he jimmied the lock and quietly opened the door. Using a pen light, he scanned the packages knowing the size he was looking for, until he came across the one with the proper address. Taking it off the shelf, he put the package into the duffle bag he was still carrying, turned out the light, and exited the mail room, closing the door and making sure it was once again locked. He then scanned the area to ensure no one was watching, and headed out a door which led to the patio.

From there he quickly made his way to Suite 14 and took a manila envelope out of the duffle bag, lifted the outside rubber guard up off the ground with the blade, and slid the package under the door.

Satisfied that this part of the mission had been completed successfully, he smiled to himself and headed toward the beach bar. Looking at his watch, he realized his men should have moved the vehicle down to the beach area by now, and he would have a slight wait if Mr. Sullivan acted as he thought he would.

Given the time he had and satisfied with what had gone on so far, he hit a number on his cell phone. Explaining where he was in the mission, he spoke to his employer.

"Yes, sir. Everything has been completed successfully so far. The package was properly mailed. I obtained the device and passed it on as agreed. And the loose end in Miami we discussed has been taken care of."

Receiving further instructions and looking at his watch, Dalton shut off the phone and put it back in his pocket and sighed. There would be no rest this night. As soon as the remainder of the mission was completed here, he would go to the airport, fly to St. Croix, and land at Henry E. Rohlsen International Airport where a limousine would pick him up and take him to Hamilton Corporate Headquarters.

His employer was known for working late hours and expected those he employed to do the same, so as Dalton arrived at the beach bar, he took a seat at the far corner, where he had an unobstructed view of the direction from which Jake Sullivan would come, ordered a Jameson neat, and waited.

CHAPTER 9

The bartender was a cute twenty-something, part Oriental, and Dalton couldn't help but notice the firmness of her young body and the revealing top and short-shorts she wore. It was flirting of a fashion. She knew he was looking, and he knew that she knew . . . a distraction to pass the time. He was trying to figure out how he would handle the situation when Jake arrived, if he arrived, when he caught a break. The bartender announced she would be back in a few minutes and that she had to take a load of glasses to the dishwasher.

Just as she left, Dalton saw Jake approaching the bar and hurried around to the bar entrance and stepped inside, right in the path of the approaching Jake.

Jake had moved up to the bar and looked around, trying to determine who had sent him the note.

Just then, the bartender, tall, in his mid-40s with sandy hair, a muscular build, and eyes that were oddly cold and removed for a bartender, even when he was smiling, approached.

"How are you doing tonight, sir? Can I get you anything?"

Jake noticed a slight accent but couldn't place it. Looking around again, he drummed his fingers on the bar and saw that the bartender was still waiting.

"Sorry. Just give me a Diet Coke."

"You got it, friend," said the bartender.

Fortunately, the cooler had glass fronts and the Diet Coke was easily found, and Dalton brought it over with a glass full of ice.

"I'm sorry to bother you, friend, but I've been asking every guy who comes in here . . . would you happen to be . . ." and he looked at the name on an envelope. "Jake Sullivan? Some guy left an envelope here earlier and asked me to give it to him."

Jake stared at the envelope in the bartender's hand.

"I am Jake Sullivan," he said, holding out his hand. "What did this guy look like?"

As Dalton turned over the envelope, he said, "Normal guy. White. Medium Build. Dark hair. Nothing out of the ordinary."

Jake turned and opened the envelope to read the note under the light from one of the tiki torches that were burning at the corners of the bar.

"Take the path to Honeymoon Beach. I will be waiting."

Slipping the note back into the envelope, Jake must have shown the concern on his face because the bartender said, "Something wrong, sir? Sir?"

Coming out of his thoughts, Jake looked at the bartender. "No, no, sorry. Everything's fine. Listen, uh, can you tell me how to get down to Honeymoon Beach?"

Giving a knowing wink, the bartender said, "Ah, here with the little lady, huh?"

Trying to end the conversation, Jake replied, "Yeah, yeah, that's it. Can you just give me the directions?"

"Oh, sure . . . sorry," said the bartender. Pointing in the direction of the bay . . . "It's right over there to the left, past the dive shop and a row of suites."

"Thanks," said Jake, reaching for the money that he carried in his front left pocket.

"Oh, sorry, Mr. Sullivan. I already got this ready for you. Just sign here and I'll put the Coke on your room."

Jake took the pen and signed the document without even looking. "Thanks for the Coke, and thanks for the information."

"Sure, Mr. Sullivan. Be careful now. Watch your step going down that path."

Dalton waited until Jake was out of sight past the dive shop and left the bar area, retrieved his duffle bag where he had stowed it in the shrubbery of a huge planter, and followed him at a distance.

Even with the cool evening breeze coming in from the Windward Passage between St. John and Lovango Cay, Jake's neck was damp with perspiration. The path was a steady grade downhill, windy in spots, and faintly illuminated with the light of the stars.

Jake was coming around another slight bend in the path when he found himself looking at five men, barely illuminated by the faint light. One appeared to be kneeling over what looked like a large garbage bag, with the other four watching. All looked in his direction when he appeared, but the way the shadows were cast in the light, Jake couldn't make out their features. He was starting to move closer when the blow on his neck fell from behind. He sensed it coming before it actually happened but couldn't move quickly enough to dodge its impact. Falling to his knees and then rolling onto his side, he saw a flutter of white, and then everything went dark.

Dalton flexed his hand after delivering the blow to Jake and stepped over his body. He then directed his attention to the other men.

"Any problems with your part of the operation?"

The one obviously in charge spoke up. "No problem at all. It was a pleasure ridding the world of this trash."

"Enough," said Dalton. "Your politics and your feelings don't interest me. This is business . . ." as he knelt down and unzipped the body bag. Looking inside, it was a black man with a goatee with deep cuts and slashes all over his body. Looking up at the leader, Dalton exploded. "What a bloody mess! You think a man like Sullivan would butcher somebody? This is supposed to be a murder . . . not a slaughter!"

The leader shrugged his shoulders. "My men got carried away. They'll be dealt with."

"If this goes south because of your stupidity, you'll be dealt with!" said Dalton. "Remember that!" Dalton looked down toward the beach where two Jeeps were parked at the entrance road. Looking at the leader and opening his duffle bag, Dalton demanded, "The weapon!"

The leader looked at the other one of his men who had been standing and motioned for him to hand something over to Dalton. The man took a sealed pouch, was about to put it into the duffle bag, when Dalton snatched it, opened it and looked at it, and turned to the two men who had come with him.

"You two . . . get the body out of that bag and leave it here on the trail. Put Sullivan inside."

The men did as they were told and one began to zip it up.

"Leave an opening at the top. I don't want him to suffocate, you idiot!"

The man glared at Dalton, but knew not to say anything and did as he was told.

Dalton directed the other man, "Head down to the beach quickly. And start the engine."

When they were finished, Dalton knelt down and lifted the bag over his shoulder with relative ease and stood. The pouch now secure in the small duffle he was carrying, he turned to head down the beach to his vehicle.

"You and your men follow me down. Get in your Jeep and get out of here. I'll take care of things from here. And no more foul ups!"

It was the leader's turn to glare at Dalton. He wasn't used to being talked to in such a fashion, but he knew that Dalton was their employer's right hand man, and he also knew Dalton was a cold blooded killer and knew it was in his best interests to accept the insult and head for the Jeep.

Never believing for a second that the men would not do what he had told them, Dalton had already started moving quickly down the beach and soon was placing the body bag holding Jake in the back of the vehicle, already thinking about the final part of the plan that was to come.

CHAPTER 10

Dalton stuck to the shadows as he maneuvered from the parked vehicle, which had made its way along the edge of the resort with its lights off, as slowly and silently as possible.

Making sure he wasn't seen, he quickly moved to Suite 14, again checked his surroundings, and opened the door with the keycard he had taken out of Jake's shorts before he had him put in the bag. Entering the room, he was guided by the one light Jake had left on. Heading for the bed, he bent forward, and lowered the bag onto it.

He quickly returned to the door and made sure it was locked and bolted, closed the blinds, and began to set the stage.

Taking Jake out of the bag, he laid him face down on the bed. After removing his shirt, shorts, and shoes – taking all the personal effects out of the shorts, which were now blood-stained, as was the shirt, from the blood that had pooled in the bag from its former occupant – he got a laundry bag from the closet and put the soiled clothes and shoes in it. These would be placed in the dumpster he would once again pass on his return trip to his vehicle.

After removing Jake's clothes, he took out a small vial and syringe and just at the base of the hairline of Jake's neck he injected a mild tranquilizer, which would keep Jake asleep until morning, when his guests would arrive.

Next, he reached into the pouch he had been given and removed what appeared to be the blade of an axe attached to a wooden handle, checked it to make sure that there was some blood stain on it, and then rubbed the blade along the inside of the body bag to make sure. Satisfied that there was enough accumulation for a lab to identify, he took the second mailing box out of his duffle bag, almost a twin of the one that had been mailed from Miami, and wrapped the blade in the day's newspaper which he also brought, as well as the package tape which he used to seal it. He looked over his handiwork.

"Another fine job by poor Alfredo," he thought, with the proper addresses and necessary information showing the package had been put into the resort's postal system for stamping and mailing this night.

Dalton smiled, remembering how easily he had entered the mail room and knew it would not be a problem to do so again.

Taking the box he had recovered out of the mail room out of his duffle bag, he opened it and removed a piece of metal that had been used to duplicate the weight of the murder weapon and put that back in his duffle bag to be disposed of later. He then put the open box in the bottom of the closet under Sullivan's carry-on, where it would be later discovered. Anyone investigating this murder would find that the murder weapon, now bearing the victim's blood, had been mailed by Jake Sullivan to Caneel Bay Resort several days before his arrival, and an attempt was made to mail it back to him the night of the murder.

Dalton smiled. "Nice planning Sullivan. Good way to avoid the TSA and get your weapon on the island." Laughing, he continued to work. Using a larger syringe he had brought, he reached into the body bag and sucked out a sizeable amount of blood. Going into the bathroom, he turned on a trickle of water in the shower and also in the sink, and using the syringe, he deposited blood in the drains of each. With such a minor flow of water, there would certainly be residue left in the elbows of the drains for the forensic techs to find.

Looking around and realizing that his work was almost done, Dalton reached into the duffle bag and pulled out a manila envelope and replaced it for the one he had put under Sullivan's door earlier. Ripping it open, he re-read the note once again to make sure everything was correct, and satisfied, he slid the note into the envelope and set it on the desk.

He had donned latex gloves prior to lifting Jake onto his shoulders and knew that fingerprints would not be a problem, but based upon his old habits, he went around the room with the towel that Sullivan had used for his shower and wiped down any surface that he thought he might have touched.

Having placed the towel back on the floor of the bathroom, he looked around the suite. Satisfied that everything was in place and that he had done what he had come to do, he quickly pulled back an edge of the drapes and looked outside and saw no one moving about. Putting Jake's keycard on the small table by the door, he took one last look, hit the switch to turn off the light, and exited.

Carrying the duffle bag in one hand with all of the items he had removed from the suite and the dirty clothes bag in the other, he retraced his steps and moved in the shadows toward the idling Jeep. Passing a dumpster approximately two hundred feet from Jake's door, he reached in and made a path with the bag of soiled clothes, stuffed it in, and re-covered it with debris.

Quickly entering the vehicle, he checked the duffle bag and everything else once again, then had the driver take him back to the entrance to the front desk.

Taking the duffle bag with him once again, he tucked one end of his shirt into his shorts and took on the gait of one who had a little too much to drink and was heading to his room to sleep it off.

Keeping his head down and barely waving to the front desk, where a new clerk was on duty, the shift having changed at midnight, as he knew, he headed out toward the suites, and as soon as he was out of sight, his posture changed and he was back to being Dalton, moving quickly to the mail room, working the lock, and entering.

Once inside, he found the section for outgoing mail and placed the mailing box in which he had placed a murder weapon covered with blood, where it soon would be found by the authorities.

Moving along the outside of the reception building, he quickly entered the vehicle and spoke to the driver.

"Let's go . . . slowly and quietly. No attention. We get to the boat . . . and we move out into open water."

They encountered no difficulty as they made their way and quickly were at the dock where the boat and its operator were waiting. Giving directions to the men in the Jeep, he watched them drive away, boarded the motor boat, and sat back.

"All right, back to the wharf in St. Thomas," he said. He put his feet up, and he leaned back his head so he could savor the cool breeze and the starry night, knowing that the plan had gone well and his employer would be pleased with the report he would give him.

CHAPTER 11

The pounding didn't fit. Jake's eyes slowly opened, the sunlight streaming on his face . . . but it couldn't be. He was in the dark, his face resting on cool sand, waves lapping at the shore.

Focusing, he realized the darkness was a dream and the sunlight was reality. Lifting his head slowly from the pillow caused a stabbing pain in the back of his head and neck. As he tried to sit, nausea swept over him. Putting his head between his legs caused the nausea to somewhat subside, and he now knew that the pounding was someone at his door.

Realizing he was wearing only underwear, he reached for his clothes, but what he wore last night was nowhere to be found. He put on one of the robes provided by the resort.

"Just a minute! Just a minute! I'm coming."

He went into the bathroom and ran cold water on his face and noticed red flecks around the drain as the water spiraled down. The pounding on the door became more intense. Last night . . . what happened? He tried to clear the cobwebs.

The pounding continued.

"Hold on! Hold on! I'm coming . . . I'm coming!" and Jake went to the door and opened it to find three dark-skinned men, two in uniform and wearing the arm patch of the U.S. Virgin Islands Police Department, with unsmiling faces standing before him.

"Mr. Sullivan?"

"Yes."

"I am Armand Lucien," said the third man dressed in a dark blue suit, obviously the leader. "I am the Zone Commander for the Special Operations Bureau of the U.S. Virgin Islands Police Department. These are Officers Delecroix and Samuelson. May we come in?"

Jake hesitated, his senses now alert, knowing that something was wrong and that it involved last night and it involved him.

"Is there a problem, Mr. Sullivan?" asked Lucien.

Jake regained his footing.

"No, come in. I'm just a little confused as to why you are here."

"Mr. Sullivan, do you know a gentleman named Andre Bollinger?" asked Lucien.

Jake was now fully alert.

"Is that recognition I see in your face, Mr. Sullivan?"

"No, no, not really," said Jake, sitting down on the edge of the bed, looking blankly ahead. "A cab driver I rode with yesterday told me about Bollinger. He's head of the PIVI?"

"Do you know him personally?" asked Lucien.

"No, no, sir. I've never met the man, never had a conversation with him ... never heard of him until yesterday when the cab driver was telling me about his run for Governor."

"Yes," said Lucien, "he was a well-known citizen of our island. He was very active in politics and concerned with the welfare of the people who live in these islands."

For some reason, Jake became irritated. "Sounds like you're a real fan, Commander."

"I would ask you to please have some respect, Mr. Sullivan," said Lucien.

Jake shook his head. "Okay, but why are you here? Wait a minute ... you're using the past tense."

"Well, Mr. Sullivan, you see, last night, Mr. Bollinger was stabbed to death . . . actually slashed . . . on the path leading down to Honeymoon Beach. Are you familiar with it?"

The path. Jake was starting to remember. Once again, Jake stared into the distance. It was coming back to him – the note under the door, the bartender and the second note, the trip down the path, the men before him, and everything going black.

"Is there something wrong, Mr. Sullivan?"

"No, no. I'm just remembering. I was there last night on that path."

At this, Lucien exchanged glances with the other two officers. "What were you doing there?"

Jake shook his head trying to focus. "When I came out of the shower last night, there was a note under the door."

The note – Jake sprung to his feet. The two officers moved quickly, hands on their weapons. Lucien waved them off. Jake headed for the desk. The envelope was still there.

"Here, here. Somebody put this under my door last night. It told me to go to the bar, which I did, and there was a bartender there, and he gave me a second envelope and the note said that someone wanted to meet me on the path to Honeymoon Beach, that they had information about associates they knew had been involved with Benjamin Matthews."

"Ah, I see. The great Benjamin Matthews case. The case I believe that first gave you your notoriety, Mr. Sullivan."

Jake stared long and hard at Lucien but didn't take the bait and didn't respond.

"And what happened while you were on the path, Mr. Sullivan?"

"I don't know. I saw five men. I was knocked out on the path. Someone hit me on the back of the head and neck and I fell. I remember my face on the path. I remember a movement of white in the moonlight . . . something moving, slowly . . . and that's all I can remember."

"And how did you arrive back at your suite, Mr. Sullivan?"

Jake shook his head. "I don't know. That's all I remember until waking up because of your pounding on my door. Look, I'm sorry for Mr. Bollinger, but I saw no murder. I'm obviously not a witness. This had to happen after . . . wait . . . maybe I was mugged, I don't know."

"Well, are all your belongings still with you?"

Jake looked around, again focusing on the desk. His wallet, keys, and other items from his pockets seemed to be there. He went over and looked. Looking in his wallet, he saw that no one had taken any money and his credit cards were all there.

"Everything appears to be here."

"So I presume we can rule out a mugging, Mr. Sullivan, since you weren't robbed in any way. You were merely assaulted by someone you can't identify after seeing five other individuals you can't identify on a path where a murder occurred last night."

"Look, I know it doesn't make sense, and I know it doesn't sound reasonable, but that's what happened."

The officer known as Delecroix approached Lucien and spoke softly to him.

"Mr. Sullivan, would you have any objection to my associate using your bathroom facilities?"

Jake sat down on the bed and waved his hand. "No, no. Go ahead." Jake sat there trying to make sense of what had occurred, when Delecroix came back and again softly spoke to the Commander.

"Mr. Sullivan, what is it that you were wearing last night?"

Jake thought for a moment. "Ah . . . I had on a pair of shorts. I think they were . . . yeah, they were tan, and I had a blue and tan tropical shirt on."

"What were you wearing on your feet?"

"Ah, Sanuks – tan and blue."

"Sanuks?" asked Lucien.

"Yeah, they're like flip-flops."

"I see," said Lucien. "Would you mind if we took a look at that clothing, Mr. Sullivan? Perhaps it would give us some evidence as to who was trying to harm you last night."

"Yeah, yeah, here . . . let me get them for you." Jake began to look around the room. "I can't . . . I can't figure this out," said Jake. "It's not here . . . they're not here . . . none of it's here. I can't find it."

"The clothes are missing, Mr. Sullivan?" asked Lucien.

"Yeah, they're not here."

"Please let me confer with my men, Mr. Sullivan, for a moment. We'll be back in just a second."

With that, Lucien and the men stepped outside. Jake began walking around the suite, looking at the items on the desk . . . looking again for his clothing . . . trying to figure out what had happened to him last night, and starting to sense that these men weren't here to investigate what had happened to him.

Just then there was a knock on the door and Jake answered, "Come in."

Lucien and the two officers walked back into the room and Jake noticed that the two officers straddled the doorway, one on each side of Lucien.

"Mr. Sullivan, would you please find some clothes and get dressed? You need to come with us to the Command Center in Cruz Bay."

"But I told you, I didn't see anything to do with the murder. I can't help you as a witness. I don't know anything."

"We don't need you as a witness, Mr. Sullivan. You're under arrest for the murder of Andre Bollinger."

"But I told you what happened!" Jake yelled. "Read the note. Feel the bump on the back of my head. Check my . . ."

"Your what, Mr. Sullivan?"

"My clothes," said Jake, "my clothes."

"Where are the clothes you wore last night, Mr. Sullivan?"

"I don't know, I told you!" yelled Jake. "Look, I don't know what's going on, but I didn't kill anybody! I don't even know this guy!"

"But you were going to meet him, were you not?"

"Of course not," said Jake. "I didn't know who I was meeting. I didn't know who wrote the note."

"Really, Mr. Sullivan?" and Lucien read the note.

"We both know what you did, Mr. Sullivan. We both know how complicit you were in the activities of Benjamin Matthews. We both know that you were a key operator in his plans to take over the government until he turned on you, and to save yourself you had to eliminate him. I have sent to you all the information I am going to in our various e-mails. Now it is time we meet. Honeymoon path. Midnight. Be there or I will take everything I know to the authorities." -- Bollinger

Incredulous, Jake cried out, "What?!" and jumped up, snatching the note from Lucien's hands, causing the two officers to move forward, again waved off by Lucien. Jake paced the suite reading the note.

"Look, this isn't the note that was in the envelope when I opened it. Someone is trying to frame me for this guy's murder. Whoever brought me back here switched the notes and put this in the envelope. Find the bartender – he gave me the second note. He was a muscular tall guy with sandy hair. Hell, he probably even saw who brought me back up the path and dumped me in my suite."

"Don't worry, Mr. Sullivan. We will continue our investigation, and we will proceed as the evidence leads us. Now, please go put on some clothes and come with us. As I stated, you're under arrest," and he began to read Jake his rights.

"I know my rights!" snapped Jake, "and I don't need them read to me."

"Ah, yes, Mr. Jake Sullivan. The famous U.S. prosecutor. So many adventures...so many important friends – even the President of the United States. Be assured, Mr. Sullivan," said Lucien, staring hard into Jake's eyes, "no strings will be pulled here for you. One of our leading citizens is dead, and our system of justice will deal with his killer. Bring him," said Lucien, as he turned on his heel and nodded to Delecroix.

CHAPTER 12

After Jake had dressed, Samuelson placed his hands behind his back, securing them with plastic cuffs, and he and Delecroix led him out the door of his suite past the startled guests and resort employees going about their daily routines in the morning sunlight. He was placed in a dark blue van with yellow police identification logos and taken to the Leander Jurgen Command, Zone D, in Cruz Bay.

Exiting the police van, Jake looked up at the three-story yellow brick building and the nightmare began to set in, like a forgotten dream being recalled after being awakened. For the first time, he felt fear at his situation, but he quickly shook it off, knowing he must steel himself and do everything in his power to stay calm and think. He was innocent. Someone for some reason was doing this. He needed all his strength and wits about him, and he needed Mike Lang.

Jake showed little or no emotion as he went through the booking procedure – photos, fingerprints. His concerns intensified when he was presented with a warrant and court order for blood for a DNA sample. He was just arrested. How could a warrant and court order have been obtained so quickly?

He was finally taken to an interrogation area and left there. Hours passed. Finally, Lucien came in carrying a cardboard box, which he gently placed on the table before he took a seat and began to speak.

Jake interrupted, "Before you start, I want a phone call and I want you to notify my attorney, U.S. Attorney Arthur Braxton, what has happened, where I am, and what the charges are – and until he gets here, I have nothing further to say to you."

Lucien leaned back in his chair and smiled. "Very well, Mr. Sullivan. I will contact your attorney, and I will give you your phone call, and you do not have to speak to me, but you will listen."

Lucien reached in and pulled a clear bag out of the box and smoothed it on the table. In it were the clothes Jake wore last night. He tried to show no emotion as Lucien turned the bag over so that Jake could clearly make out the blood stains on the front of the shirt and shorts.

"Mr. Sullivan, I am happy to report to you that we found the clothing you wore last night. It was stuffed into the bottom of a dumpster less than 200 feet from your suite. Shirt, pants, and . . . ah, yes . . . those a . . . Sanuks, as you called them. I'm afraid all are somewhat damaged with what appears to be blood stains. We are comparing Mr. Bollinger's DNA with the blood and, of course, your DNA with the blood, to determine whose it might be."

Shaking his head as a parent might while trying to educate a child, Lucien pulled out another plastic bag with what appeared to be a sheet of plain white paper.

"Mr. Sullivan, this is a note we found on Mr. Bollinger's body, along with an envelope which appears to have been mailed to him from Miami several days ago. As you can see, the note asks for a meeting during your trip to St. John and, therefore, it appears that you are the person who set up this meeting. Take a look at it, Mr. Sullivan, if you would please. Is that not your signature at the bottom?"

Jake read the note.

"Bollinger, I've had enough of your e-mails and your threats. It is time we meet face to face. You already know when I'm coming to St. John. Contact me and we'll meet and resolve this once and for all."

At the bottom was a signature that Jake recognized as clearly his own.

He sat back . . . trying to think . . . trying to remember . . . and then it came to him. He looked at Lucien.

"The bartender. He put something in front of me and asked me to sign it . . . told me it was my bar bill . . . but I really didn't look at it. That's when I signed this note."

"Really, Mr. Sullivan?" said Lucien. "But the note was in an envelope postmarked several days ago."

"Look, I can't explain it. It's all part of the setup. I'm telling you, that's how they got my signature."

"I see," said Lucien, nodding his head and taking back the note and setting it on the desk.

Still smiling, Lucien pulled out a third bag, holding what appeared to be some type of cutting implement with an axe-like blade. The blade was inset into a wooden handle, which had a carving of a leaf set deep into the wood.

"This is a unique instrument, Mr. Sullivan. I thought you might recognize it. It's called a chiveta. It's used to cut tobacco leaf. Funny thing is it looks very, very familiar to one you received several years ago for your work in ridding Ybor City in Florida of a very bad criminal gang, as I understand it." Lucien slid the newspaper photograph and article toward Jake. "The peculiar thing is, Mr. Sullivan, we found this implement in a mailing box to be readied for the outgoing mail at the resort." Lucien pulled the small box out of the bigger box, again protected by plastic, and pushed it toward

Jake. "As you can see, the address to which the box is to be mailed is yours. What? No comment, Mr. Sullivan?"

Using everything in his being, Jake controlled his emotions, trying to show no outward appearance that he knew where this evidence was leading and how damning it was as to his guilt or innocence.

"Oh, by the way, Mr. Sullivan, we obtained additional warrants to search your computer files and your office. My agents are on their way to Miami. As a matter of fact, they should be arriving there shortly. Hopefully, we will be able to determine the whereabouts of the chiveta in this picture, as I'm sure you keep it somewhere in your home or office."

"Quit playing games Lucien. The one I received came with a stand – it's sitting on the credenza behind my desk."

"Mr. Sullivan, please, you indicated you do not want to speak. I do not want to infringe upon your rights. We will see . . . we will see."

Next, Lucien removed another box and placed it on the table.

"This is an odd thing, Mr. Sullivan. This box, which we found in the bottom of your closet, bears post office markings that indicate it was mailed by you in Miami to the Caneel Bay Resort here in St. John several days ago. The box was weighed. We took the box and put the chiveta into it and the weight is identical to the weight shown on the package."

Lucien then pulled a folder out of the box and again sat it on the table between him and Jake.

"This folder contains a statement from two witnesses, a husband and wife, who were heading down Honeymoon path when a man almost knocked them over running by them up the path. They said he was wearing a floral shirt, blue and tan, and tan shorts. His description, build, height . . . match yours, Mr. Sullivan. His clothes were blood stained. As they proceeded down the path somewhat further, they came across the body of Mr. Bollinger. They saw no one else on the path. They certainly didn't see anybody knocked out lying on the path, or any other men whatsoever. I'm surprised, Mr. Sullivan. For all your fame and acclaim, you did a very poor job in hiding your crime. CSU removed blood from your sink and shower drain – I'm sure it will be a match to Mr. Bollinger, as will the blood on your clothes. We recovered finger prints from the chiveta handle, and I'm sure those fingerprints will be yours. I'm sure my agents in Miami will find that your chiveta is no longer in your office, as you mailed it to yourself . . . meaning, Mr. Sullivan that this crime . . . this murder of our citizen . . . was premeditated . . . . that you planned this because he was going to expose you for what you really are . . . a criminal."

The anger in Jake continued to rise but he said nothing, staring hard at Lucien as he went on. One by one, slowly putting the bags and items back in the box, all the time smiling at Jake, Lucien finally sighed.

"Oh, yes, there is one more thing, Mr. Sullivan. There was no male bartender at the beach bar last night, and the young lady tending bar never saw you."

Putting a lid on the box, Lucien rose, still smiling. He took a handkerchief from his back pocket and wiped his hands, carefully folded the handkerchief back up, and put it back in his pocket, and once again smiled at Jake.

"I'll show in Mr. Braxton when he arrives, Mr. Sullivan."

Jake had been sitting silently through it all, knowing each piece of evidence built a solid case, something that Jake had done all his life. Trying to hide his knowledge of how well this had been planned and how thorough were those who had planned it, he became angry and determined, and just as the door began to open he growled, "Sit down Lucien!"

The smile on Lucien's face departed. He knew the lack of rank and the manner of address was an affront to him, but he let it pass. Sitting the box on the table, he retook his seat.

Leaning in as close as he could to Lucien's face, Jake began, "I don't know whether it's your ego or lack of intelligence that is driving you, or if there is something else involved, but let me make myself clear . . . this, for reasons I do not know but will find out, is an elaborate attempt to frame me for a murder I did not commit. I will get to the bottom of this, and so help me, I will destroy everyone . . . and I mean everyone . . . who is a part of it."

The implication was not lost on Lucien, and Jake could see the hatred and contempt in his eyes, but Lucien remained calm. He rose, picked up the box, and turned to the door. Before exiting, he looked back at Jake.

"This is not one of those adventure novels where you see yourself as the hero. There is no cabal, no conspiracy against you, no one is framing you. You will soon be revealed as the criminal you are – as a murderer who killed to cover his crimes and maintain his famous persona, and you will pay the ultimate price." And with that, he closed the door and was gone.

CHAPTER 13

Fifteen minutes later U.S. Attorney Arthur Braxton entered the interrogation room.

"Christ Jake! What the hell is going on?"

"I'm being framed for murder, that's what's going on."

"Jake, you know better than anyone the Justice Department is prosecutorial. We don't defend criminal cases."

"I don't want you to defend me. I want you to take over the prosecution."

"What?!" said Braxton in disbelief.

"Look," said Jake, "I'm being framed and I don't know by whom, but whomever it is, he has resources and a well-conceived, thought-out plan. It's elaborate in its details. I know damn well what they're calling the murder instrument used to be sitting in my office in Miami. They have a box showing I mailed it to myself here. And they found the damn thing in a box that was going to be mailed back to me in Miami."

Quickly going over the details of what happened the night before, Jake concluded, "Whoever brought me back took my clothes off, hid them in a dumpster, made sure some of the blood from the crime scene was in the shower drain and my sink drain, changed the note that had been shoved under my door, and I would bet anything that the DNA they find in the blood on my clothes and the weapon is going to be that of this Bollinger, and my fingerprints are going to be all over it."

"Wow Jake. You know how few times I've gotten cases with evidence that's that good?"

Jake stared at Braxton. "Not exactly words I want to hear right now, Art."

Braxton started apologizing.

"Forget it. I know. I know. I told you, this is a well-thought-out, elaborate frame. One other thing, Art. I think somewhere in the chain of authority somebody's in on this. The court order and warrant for DNA and the boys being sent off to Miami came way too quick in this case. It was like everything was ready to go and put into place before the event even happened."

"Jake, do you have any evidence or proof of any kind as to who would want to do this to you and why?"

"That's the part I don't understand, Art. Obviously, someone wanted to get rid of Bollinger, and that could be a lot of people . . . but why frame me? Why me? They could have had this guy killed by anybody on these islands. There are a lot of people who don't want him around. This frame wasn't just about killing Bollinger . . . it was about putting me away for his murder. Look, Art . . . I need to get this into federal jurisdiction. Get the U.S. Marshals down here and get me on a plane to Miami, and get me some time to figure this out. This guy Lucien is ramrodding this thing. He's convinced he's got a big fish, and he's going to push it as hard as he can."

"But Jake, how do we get this turned over to Miami?"

"Look, they served a warrant in Miami for the hard drives on my computer and this knife business. If they're saying I used the U.S. Mail to send a murder weapon here, that gives us jurisdiction anywhere in the federal system, particularly in Miami where it was mailed from."

"Okay," said Braxton, "I'll buy it. That'll work. But Jake . . ."

"Look Art . . . I know on its face the evidence is overwhelming. I'm telling you I didn't do this, and I'm asking for your help. It's your call."

Braxton sat back, lifted his hands, slowly shook his head, and then looked up at Jake. "What the hell . . . it's only my career. Alright, here's what we do. Judge Ashby is not in court until Monday. I think he went to the States for some judicial meeting, so I can't get a writ of habeas corpus until then. I'll keep on track of what they find out from the warrant they sent to Miami whenever they get here. I'll file a discovery request and personally give it to Lucien and file with the local court. When Ashby signs the writ, I'll have Marshals standing by. You waive extradition to Miami, and we get you home. Jake, you do know that if we do this, we will have to prosecute unless you can clear yourself . . . and like we said, on the evidence, it's one hell of a case."

"I know," said Jake, "but I'll take my chances. I'm not going to trust my life to the system here."

"You're right not to," said Braxton. "The Presiding Judge of the Superior Court in the Virgin Islands is the Honorable Emmit Denton, an old bastard, mean as hell, and supposedly on the take. He hears every criminal case in the islands. Let's just say his decisions are sometimes hard to understand and correlate with the law. And the Chief Prosecutor, a guy named Donaldson . . ."

Jake interrupted. "The guy that ran for Governor?"

"Yeah, the same. He's supposedly even a bigger crook."

"Great," said Jake. "Where is the local court around here?"

"The Alexander A. Farrelly Justice Center, right next door to us on Veterans Drive."

Jake shook his head. "Paradise my ass."

"Look Jake," said Braxton, "we'll get the writ approved. We'll get you out of here."

"Yeah, but I still have to clear myself. Thanks Art. I appreciate you going out on a limb for me."

"No problem Jake. I've know you too long. You're not a murderer . . . a pain in the ass, but not a murderer."

Jake smiled. "One more thing. I'm calling Kirkland. I have to tell him what's going on and tell him to get Mike Lang down here now."

"I understand. I'll see you Monday."

Shortly thereafter a guard came in and took Jake to a phone hanging on the wall and told him how to place his call. After he told what he could to Kirkland in the allotted three minutes, he was escorted back to his cell. Exhausted, Jake laid down on the stone bench, but he didn't sleep. The time for sleep and worry and fear was over. The adrenaline was there. He had a case to solve, a puzzle to put together, and a murderer to find. He had to start connecting the dots. He had to get ready for Mike.

MIAMI, FLORIDA
U.S.A.

CHAPTER 14

It was a slow afternoon in Miami. A thick blanket of rain clouds had come in from the Atlantic and a steady drizzle pinged the windows. Mike Lang was working on the quarterly reports due at the end of March. More paperwork he hated. Eva came in. Mike could tell from her face that something was wrong.

"Mike, there are two investigators here. They are from the U.S. Virgin Islands Police Department. They want to search Jake's office and confiscate his hard drive."

"What the hell?" said Mike, pushing away from the desk.

Coming into the outer office, he saw two men in suits standing at attention.

"Cops, no doubt about it," thought Mike. "What's this all about, gentlemen?"

The answer to his question was one of the agents handing him a piece of paper. Mike looked it over. They were clearly warrants and a subpoena issued by the Superior Court of the U.S. Virgin Islands. Finally, one of the two agents spoke.

"As you can see, these give us the right to search the office of one Jake Sullivan and confiscate his computer hard drives."

"Okay, wait a minute," said Mike. "What's this all about? Has something happened to Jake? What's going on?"

"I'm sorry, we cannot reveal the nature of our investigation at this time."

"Bullshit! You stay right there. I'm going to talk to someone who can tell me what's going on. Eva, get me . . ." and she was already on the phone, holding up her hand to Mike in a waiting motion.

"Yes, sir, they are. Yes, sir, he is. Right away, sir. Hold on. Mike, it's Lester Kirkland. There's something wrong with Jake. He wants to talk to you right now."

Mike went back in the office, picked up the receiver, and pushed the button. "Les, what the hell is going on? What's with Jake, and why are two cops here from the Virgin Islands with warrants and subpoenas?"

"Mike listen carefully. This is a very serious situation for both Jake and the administration. Honor the warrants and subpoenas and get those two out of the office and call me back."

"What? You've gotta be kidding me," said Mike.

"Mike, I know your nature, but believe me, this is a potentially disastrous situation and for once I need you to do exactly what I tell you . . . you understand?"

"Yeah, but . . ."

"Mike . . ."

"All right, all right. I will. And believe me, I will call you as soon as their asses are out of here."

Mike went out of the office. "Go to it boys. Remember – you break anything, you pay for it."

Without even a hint of a smile, the men moved into Jake's office, worked quickly, and in less than an hour, they photographed the office, scanned documents, removed hard drives, provided Mike with a list of what they had taken, and then they were gone. The door to the outer office barely closed behind them when Mike was back on the phone with Kirkland.

"All right, the Bobbsey Twins are gone after turning Jake's office inside out. What the hell is going on?"

Mike, I want you to know I've got Jason Bates here, also, and you're on speaker phone.

"Jason, don't take this the wrong way, but whenever you're around, that means something somewhere has gone to hell."

"Very perceptive, as usual, Mr. Lang," said Jason Bates, President Fletcher's Chief of Staff. "I suggest you save the humor and be quiet and listen to what Mr. Kirkland has to tell you."

"Mike, what do you know about the political situation in the Virgin Islands?"

"Hell, Les, I don't even follow politics here. You know that."

"Point taken. All right, let me give you the nickel tour. The Territorial Governor of the U.S. Virgin Islands is one James Sterling, who won a very close election against two other opponents with the formal backing, influence, and money of President Fletcher and the party. One of the opponents was Andre Bollinger, who was found murdered on a beach path below the Caneel Bay Resort last night/early this morning. Bollinger was the head of the PIVI – the Party for the Independence of the Virgin Islands – and a sworn antagonist of President Fletcher. The other candidate was the Chief Criminal Prosecutor for the Superior Court of the Virgin Islands."

"You going to tell me soon how this relates to Jake?"

"I'm about to. Mike, Jake was arrested this morning and charged with the murder of Andre Bollinger."

"What?! Are you out of your mind? What the hell are you talking about?" said Mike.

"Mike, calm down and listen. We obviously know that Jake is innocent, but there is a huge amount of evidence piling up against him. Whoever is framing him is doing so elaborately, carefully, and with a great deal of planning."

"And what are we gonna to do about it?" said Mike.

"That is the point, Mike. We . . . the government . . . can't do anything about it."

"You've gotta be kidding me! You're gonna let Jake . . ."

"Wait wait, Mike, wait. Listen to me. I just told you, Bollinger and the President were more than just adversaries. With the current situation in Congress, this whole independence movement has become a political football. We now have a situation where someone who has worked closely with the President and on his behalf in several high-profile situations is accused of murdering the President's chief political opponent in a U.S. territory. The President . . ."

Then Bates spoke up. "Mike, the President can be in no way seen as doing anything to interfere with the investigation or prosecution. If this thing blows up, it would be political suicide."

"Jason, what the hell do you mean 'if it blows up'? Do you actually think that Jake did this?"

"Of course not, but that doesn't mean that he can't be convicted."

"And you're just gonna let that happen?"

"No, we're not going to just let that happen. The President wants you to go to the Virgin Islands, find out who's framing Jake, and obtain the necessary evidence to get him released, and if possible, to find out who the true culprit is so that the U.S. Attorney in the Virgin Islands can begin prosecution."

"So you're telling me I'm supposed to go save Jake's ass and with no help from you?"

"It's worse than that Mike," said Kirkland.

"Listen Mike," said Bates, "understand this carefully. You will be going to the Virgin Islands as a United States citizen, a friend of Jake Sullivan, and not as his investigator in the Justice Department. You will not have any resources from the Justice Department in this matter. Jake has already asked Arthur Braxton, the U.S. Attorney, to take over the prosecution of the case."

"Jake wants to be prosecuted?" asked Mike.

"Think about it, Mike. He wants to get this into a situation where we can change jurisdictions, bring him back to Miami for prosecution, delay the prosecution until we have time to sort this out, investigate, and find out what the hell is really going on. The Justice Department can't defend someone convicted of murder in a capital case that has interstate complications like this one allegedly does. They can only prosecute. Jake knows that, so that is what he's asking Braxton to do."

"Okay," said Mike. "Let me get this straight. While Braxton is doing what he needs to do legally to get Jake out of jail and transferred to jail in Miami to be prosecuted for murder in Miami, I'm supposed to find out who framed him for that murder in the Virgin Islands. Is that the plan?"

"That's basically it," said Kirkland.

"And I can't count on anybody from your end to give us any help whatsoever?"

"Again, correct."

"Jason, do I need to repeat what occurs when you're involved in these things?"

"Yes, Mike – I know. And I have to tell you one other thing."

"This oughta be good," said Mike.

"If you in any way break the law while you're doing this and you're arrested in the Virgin Islands, we can't come to your rescue, and we can't send anyone else to help Jake. So, you're going to have to do this and follow the rules. Go by the book. Don't step on anyone's toes."

"You mean conduct one of my normal investigations?"

"Actually," said Kirkland, "he's talking about anything but."

"Anything else I need to know?" said Mike.

"Look, here's what we'll do. If we get any more information in our hands, we'll get it to Eva. Give her a number where she can reach you, and we'll provide you with as much intelligence and information as we can. Other than that, Mike, I'm afraid you're on your own."

"Okay, Les. I get it. Let me get on it."

"One more thing," said Bates.

"I'm almost afraid to ask," said Mike. "What?"

"I've a message for Jake."

"And what is it you want to tell him?" asked Mike.

"Not from me . . . from the President of the United States. He knows Jake's innocent. He knows he's been framed. He's deeply sorry that he can take no action on Jake's behalf, but he has the utmost faith in you . . . otherwise, he wouldn't put Jake's fate in your hands."

"I'll tell Jake," said Mike, "and I appreciate it. But I also know that the President knows no matter what he told me to do, what you told me to do, or what Les told me to do, I'm on the next plane to the Virgin Islands, and I will get Jake out of this."

Bates replied, "I think that thought did cross the President's mind. Good luck, Mike."

And with that, the line went dead.

Mike slowly hung up the phone and looked out the window in Jake's office. "Well, at least they didn't say the tape would self-destruct. For Jake's sake, I hope it's not mission impossible. Eva! Can you come in? Here's the situation. Jake's been falsely accused of murdering a political big shot down in the Virgin Islands."

"Oh my God!" said Eva.

"I know. I know. The good news is I'm going down there and, as usual, get him out of trouble. The bad news is Bates, Kirkland, and the rest can't help us on this one. The guy that was killed was involved in politics, and since Jake's so close to the President, he can't be seen as interfering in an on-going investigation."

"So what you're saying is . . . it's on you . . . right?"

"Looks that way, Eva."

"Well, I personally wouldn't want it any other way. What do we need to do?"

"First, get me on the next flight to the Virgin Islands. Second, here's a list of names that I want you to get me as much information as you can on before I leave. The guy that was killed was named Andre Bollinger. He's the head of this party . . . the PIVI . . . he tries to promote independence for the Virgin Islands, and he's an adversary of President Fletcher. I need to call the U.S. Attorney down there. His name's Arthur Braxton. I'll see if I can get some information from him . . . if I can get any names about who's involved – I want you to look up them, too. The rest I'll have to play by ear when I get down there."

"I'll get on it right away, Mike." Eva got up and headed for the door, where she turned. "Looks like you were right, Mike. Jake should have taken you with him."

"He'll never learn," said Mike. "Hey, when you get out there, get me Braxton on the phone."

"I'm on it," said Eva, and she was gone.

Within minutes the intercom buzzed and Mike picked up.

"U.S. Attorney Arthur Braxton is on the line, Mike."

"Thanks, Eva. Hello . . . Mr. Braxton?"

"Yeah Mike. Please call me Art."

"All right Art. What's going on down there?"

Mike sat and listened as Braxton went over everything regarding the arrest, the evidence, and what he planned to do on Monday morning.

"What do you think the odds are on getting him out and getting him back here?"

97

"I think they're good. It's clearly an interstate matter with the alleged weapon coming from Miami to the Virgin Islands. I don't think Judge Ashby will have any problem agreeing to a writ of habeas corpus and putting it into the federal system. If I may ask," said Braxton, "what are you going to do when you get down here?"

"I'm going to find out who did this and clear Jake's name. I agree with getting him into the federal system – it will protect him and give us time – but I still have to clear him."

"Agreed," said Braxton. "Well, based upon your resumé, I certainly wouldn't mind having you on my side."

"Thanks Art. Listen, can you get me a copy of the case file? I'd like to review it on my way down there, if I could."

"Yeah, as a matter of fact, the guy in charge, a guy named Lucien, just sent it over to me. Be careful with him, Mike. He's a real by-the-book guy, and I think he's gunning for Jake."

"Too bad," said Mike, "doesn't sound like we'll be friends."

"Listen Mike, keep in touch when you get down here. I'll help in any way I can."

"Thanks Art. I appreciate it, but this is one you might want to stay away from other than what you're doing."

"Yeah, I figured the powers that be would back off from this, given the situation . . . especially with Jake's relationship with the President, but I'll still help in any way I can. I've known Jake a long time, and I'd like to keep on top of this."

"All right, I'll keep you posted. Soon as I know anything, I'll let you know."

"Alright Mike . . . I'll get you those files."

"Thanks Art," and with that, he hung up.

Mike called out the door. "Eva! Add another name to the list . . . a guy named Lucien. He's the cop in charge of this down in the Virgin Islands. See what you can find out about him."

Eva stuck her head in the doorway. "I already got some information on the other stuff you gave me. I'll get on top of that right now. Anything else you need . . . just let me know. Anything to help Jake."

"I know, Eva. Thanks."

Mike turned his chair toward the window and stared at the inclement weather. "Yeah Jake, all your friends want to help. I just hope it's enough."

ST. THOMAS
ST. JOHN
U.S. V.I.

CHAPTER 15

It was late Thursday night when Mike arrived in St. Thomas. Grabbing a cab, he followed the same path Jake had taken and got on the shuttle at Red Hook and arrived in Cruz Bay a little after 11:00 P.M. He immediately grabbed a cab at the ferry terminal that dropped him off at the Westin St. John Resort, where Eva had been able to get him a room for the next several days.

After he checked in, he went to his room and opened his duffel bag. He took out the $50,000.00 in cash he had taken from the temporary evidence storage facility that was part of the evidence from a drug raid and had yet to be logged in and transported to the evidence room. He knew there'd be hell to pay, but he'd worry about that later. He was in the islands and he was going to need cash to get done what he had to get done.

Removing one of the ceiling tiles in the entranceway of his room, he secured the packet of money and replaced the tile. He looked around the room to make sure that everything was as it should be, making sure he had left certain items at certain angles so he would know if they had been touched and his room had been searched.

After deciding that everything was as he wanted it, he made his way to the front desk and called for a cab and headed for the Command Center where Jake was being held.

CHAPTER 16

Jake tossed and turned on the thin mattress he had been given as he replayed in his mind over and over again what had happened, looking for any clue that could lead him to finding the person or persons who had framed him, but every time he went over all that he knew, he kept running into walls that he couldn't get around or go over. Finally, he had enough. He sat up, threw off the blanket that still had a slight odor of urine and human sweat that found its way through the overpowering smell of commercial detergent. He went and sat on the stone bench, his head between his hands, and tried to come up with a new way to attack the evidence.

Just then, he heard sounds out in the hallway and looked up, and for the first time since early the night before, he smiled, as Mike Lang stood on the other side of the bars. The officer on duty opened the cell and motioned for Mike to enter.

"You have fifteen minutes."

"Look, give us a break pal. I just got here. Let me talk to him for a while."

"Fifteen minutes," and the jailer walked away.

Mike walked in and leaned against the wall. "Can't say much for the help."

"Yeah, but look at the accommodations," said Jake, moving his hand around the extent of the cell, as if showing a finely appointed hotel suite. They both smiled. Mike broke the silence.

"You know, if you had told me you were going to come down here to kill somebody, I wouldn't have been so upset you didn't bring me with you."

Jake looked up. "Well, you know, it was sort of spur of the moment."

"Not according to the file I read," said Mike.

"All right wise-ass," said Jake. "Tell me what you really think."

"I think someone's gone to a lot of trouble to frame you for this guy's murder. Have you been able to come up with any connection at all?"

"Nothing Mike. Nothing. I never met the guy, I never talked to the guy, I was never involved in any of Fletcher's dealings down here . . . nothing."

"How about any of our old cases?"

"I can't come up with anything."

"Well," said Mike, "I have Eva checking the files. If she finds any connection, she'll let us know. What about Bollinger?"

"Obviously," said Jake, "someone wanted him taken out, and I imagine there are a lot of people on that list."

"But you are the key here, Jake. They could've gotten to Bollinger any number of ways. Hell, they could have paid some local to kill him, hired a hit man, made him have an accident, made it look like a heart attack. There's all kinds of ways to do it. But they wanted a very, very public murder, and they wanted it to involve you."

"Maybe we're looking at this the wrong way," said Jake. "Maybe we're focusing too much on the islands. Maybe we should go back and look through all the cases."

Mike shook his head. "No, there's a tie-in here. This happened here for a reason. My best guess . . . it's someone who's had a long-standing grudge against you, who, for whatever reason, also bene-fited from Bollinger's death. They found out you were coming here and decided that's when they'd take him out and frame you for the job. And there's a political element to this, too, Jake," said Mike. And he went over everything he talked about with Kirkland and Bates, including the message from the President they asked he deliver to Jake.

"Well, it's nice to know the President of the United States doesn't think I'm a murderer, but basically, what you're telling me is that we're on our own, huh?"

"Yeah. That's the other part of this setup. I read the informa-tion Eva could get together for me in the short time she had while I was on the plane coming down here. Let me run this by you and you tell me what you think. Somebody wants to take out Bollinger – that means they want to hurt the PIVI. They frame you for one of two reasons, or both. One, somebody has a grudge against you and it's personal; or, two, they use you because you are publicly known as being close to President Fletcher. So, your arrest makes him look bad. Now, when the next election for Governor comes, who benefits?"

Jake thought about it. "Well, if the PIVI is demoralized, lost its leadership and its mouthpiece, and if Fletcher's candidate, the current Governor, suffers, the guy that benefits is Donaldson, the prosecutor."

"Exactly," said Mike. "From what I understand, there was a lot of money from some unknown conglomerate behind him."

Jake stood up. "Yeah, and what he primarily campaigned on was reopening the oil refinery on St. Croix."

Mike looked at Jake. "Greed's always a good reason for murder."

"So, maybe, it's not personal. Maybe it's just because of my political ties with Fletcher."

"It is possible," said Mike, "but my gut tells me there's something else to it."

"So where do we go from here?" asked Jake.

"While I'm here, I'm going to try and see the girl who was bartending Wednesday night and then I'm going back to the room to get some sleep and get up early in the morning. I'm already booked on the 6:00 A.M. ferry to Red Hook. I'll take a cab to the airport. I'm booked on the 8:59 Cape Air flight to St. Croix. I want to talk to the witnesses who allegedly saw you coming up the hill. They live and work on the island, so hopefully, I can catch them at work and get both their statements. Anything else from your friends here?"

"No. Lucien hasn't been back to give me any more gleeful findings regarding the evidence."

"Eva couldn't get much info on him, but everything she did get seems to indicate he's clean . . . a real stickler for procedure . . . but clean."

"Oh, he's a stickler for procedure alright. But I have a feeling someone else is pulling the strings, Mike. This happened way too quickly and way too smoothly for a local island police force."

"I'll keep digging and see what I can find," said Mike. "Hopefully, I'll be back to see you tomorrow with good news from St. Croix."

"Yeah, that'd be nice. I could use some good news."

Just then the guard came back. "Time's up"

"That's okay, pal," said Mike. "I was just leaving anyway." He turned and looked at Jake. "Hang in there. I'll find out who did this."

"Hey, I'm not going anywhere," said Jake.

Just then the jailer shut the door and turned the key back in the lock. Just as Mike started to move down the hallway, Jake called out.

"Mike!"

"Yeah, what is it Jake?"

"Linda and the girls . . ."

"I already talked to them," said Mike. "I explained all the circumstances and what's going on here. They gave me a message for you, too. They love you, and they know you're not a murderer, and they know together you and I will get you out of this."

Jake nodded his head. "Thanks for coming down here, Mike."

Mike smiled. "Sure, now you're happy to see me."

In spite of the circumstances, Jake had to laugh. And with that, Mike was gone.

CHAPTER 17

Before going back to his hotel room that night, Mike followed up on what he told Jake and took a chance the same bartender would be working at the beach bar at Caneel Bay. He got a cab there and a very kind staff member showed him the way to the bar.

Sitting down, he saw that the bartender was a pretty, young girl who matched the description contained in Jake's file, which Arthur Braxton, true to his word, had sent over before Mike left Florida.

She came over to ask Mike if he wanted a drink. He ordered a cold Corona with no lime and introduced himself.

Julia Chen was a student at UCLA taking time off to bartend in paradise. She'd been working at this bar every spring for the past three years, and she was working Wednesday night. Unfortunately, she confirmed that there was no male bartender working the shift and she never saw Mr. Sullivan at the bar. She indicated that she worked from 5:00 P.M. until 2:00 A.M., closing time, and saw nothing out of the ordinary – no suspicious persons, no one carrying or dragging someone up the path from Honeymoon Beach, and in fact, it was a pretty quiet night. However, she did provide one interesting fact. Around midnight, she announced to the bar that she had to take a load of glasses in for washing and bring clean ones back and would be gone for about 15 minutes. That was approximately the time Jake would have been at the bar, and enough time for someone to slip in, pretend to be the bartender, and send Jake on his way. But once again, there was no proof.

Mike got directions from Julia and walked down the path to the beach and saw one of the resort Jeeps come down an access road to his right and park. "That's why no one saw Jake going up the path," thought Mike. "They took him down the beach and loaded him into a car and drove him back to the suite. They unloaded him and then set everything up."

ST. THOMAS
ST. CROIX
U.S. V.I.

CHAPTER 18

The 8:10 Cape Air flight from St. Thomas to St. Croix took off on time. Mike had booked the 3:00 o'clock P.M. flight back, figuring he would be back in enough time to catch the 5:30 P.M. ferry back to St. John.

The plane touched down at the Henry E. Rohlsen International Airport, named for a St. Croix native who was one of the Tuskegee Airmen. In reviewing the file, Mike knew that Mrs. Andrea Burke worked as a lab technician at Hamilton Laboratories in Aldersville, just outside of Christiansted, and that Mr. Marcus Burke was a CPA who worked in the corporate offices of Hamilton Industries in Christiansted.

Mike caught a cab, gave the cabbie the address in Aldersville, and they headed out onto the Melvin Evans Highway, which would take them to Route 70 for the six-mile ride. Traffic was light on the road, and out of habit, Mike turned periodically to check the traffic moving behind him. He took note of a non-descript gray sedan keeping a steady distance behind the cab. Mike saw a sign up ahead showing an exit for Spanishtown. He reached up and tapped the cabbie on the shoulder.

"Turn off here, now."

"But sir, it's not . . ."

"Do what I say! Turn off!"

Quickly the cabbie jerked the wheel to the right, just catching the exit.

"Slow down and pull over," he directed again.

The cabbie, shaking his head, pulled the cab over to the side of the road and stopped, looking in the rear-view mirror quizzically.

"Just sit here for a few minutes. Don't worry, I'll pay you for your time."

It was only a moment before the gray sedan passed them, continuing down the exit ramp and making a right onto a side road.

"Well," thought Mike to himself, "someone knows I'm here, and someone wants to find out where I'm going."

"Okay, let's get back on the highway and get me to my destination."

"It's your dollar, man," said the cabbie, driving past the side road where the gray car had turned to the right. It was nowhere to be seen.

They arrived at Hamilton Laboratories in Aldersville without further incident. Mike saw no more vehicles trailing them and the gray car did not appear again.

After Mike entered the main building, he was met by a guard and escorted into a room and asked to wait.

Presently, a thin, young woman with short cut auburn hair and a white lab coat, wearing glasses, entered the room, accompanied by a tall man with sandy hair.

"Mr. Lang?" the man said.

"Mike Lang. And you are?"

"My name is Mr. Dalton. I'm head of security for Hamilton Industries, and this is Mrs. Andrea Burke."

"How did you know I was going to be here today . . . and how did you know I wanted to speak to Mrs. Burke?"

"Commander Lucien was kind enough to give us a call. He indicated you had arrived on the island and, in all probability, would want to speak to the witnesses. It just so happens that I came out here today to speak with Mr. and Mrs. Burke to explain to them who you are and that you might be coming to interview them."

Now Mike knew why he had been followed. They were keeping watch for him at the airport. The car following was to let Mr. Dalton know exactly how far away he was so he had sufficient time to prep the witness.

Mike held out his hand. "Mrs. Burke, I'm pleased to meet you. If I may ask is there a security issue here I don't know about?"

"You have to understand, Mr. Lang," said Mr. Dalton, "this event has caused great concern throughout the entire islands. We are not used to having public figures murdered, and the fact that Mr. and Mrs. Burke are the ones who discovered the body has made them the subjects of much unwanted attention. The news media around the world is trying to contact them to get information, and there even have been threats made against them by parties unknown. Obviously, we here at Hamilton Industries are determined to ensure the safety and well-being of our employees. When we learned you were here, Mrs. Burke asked me to sit in on this meeting, and I readily agreed."

"So what you're telling me is that I can't question Mrs. Burke about the statement she made to the police in private?"

"She would prefer that not be the case, and since you have no real official capacity in this investigation, I would suggest that her wishes be honored."

"Let's get to it," said Mike. "Please have a seat, Mrs. Burke."

"I'll just sit over here in the corner, if you don't mind," said Dalton.

"Whether or I mind or not doesn't seem to matter," said Mike.

Dalton gave Mike a cold, hard stare, which Mike held until Dalton looked away. Then Mike began to go over the statement with Mrs. Burke. He was more concerned with what she hadn't said than what she had. He asked about things that were not covered in the statement, such as the position of the hands, the feet, whether the body was on its back or on its front, in which direction was the head positioned. He could see that Mrs. Burke was becoming more and more alarmed as he went on, afraid she would say the wrong thing. She was constantly gazing over at Dalton, as if she was pleading for him to intervene, but Mike had a sense as to when that intervention would come, and he ended the interview before it did.

"Thank you, Mrs. Burke. I appreciate your time in going over everything again. I'm sure this was hard for you with everything that you've gone through, and I truly appreciate it."

Mike decided it was time to take a shot. "I presume you brought Mr. Burke here from the corporate offices with you and I can interview him next." Mike could tell he caught Dalton off guard, but he quickly recovered.

"I didn't know you were coming, Mr. Lang, but since I was coming down here to interview Mrs. Burke I decided to bring Mr. Burke with me so that I could go over their statements together at the same time."

"I'm sure that was convenient for you," said Mike, "but I'd like to interview Mr. Burke separately without Mrs. Burke present, if you don't mind."

"I'm sorry, Mr. Lang. I can sense that Mrs. Burke is upset by this whole affair, and I think she would be more comfortable if she was with her husband," and he stared at Mrs. Burke, who quickly got the message.

"Yes, that's true, Mr. Dalton. I would feel much more comfortable if I could be with my husband now. This whole matter is very upsetting."

Mike sat back in his chair. "I'm happy to accommodate you in any way that I can, Mrs. Burke. Mr. Dalton, if you don't mind, would you bring in Mr. Burke?"

Mike changed the scope of his interview, focusing with Mr. Burke on the elements of his statement, until the very end, when he suddenly veered off to body positioning and the other factors that had so disrupted his wife.

And then it happened. When he had asked Mrs. Burke in which position the head was pointing, she had said up the hill toward the resort. When he asked Mr. Burke, he said the head was pointing down the hill toward the beach, an error which Mrs. Burke quickly corrected.

"No, honey, you are mistaken. Don't you remember? We thought that poor man must have been coming up the hill because his body was lying with his head facing up toward the resort. It wasn't toward the beach."

Burke looked at her, and then at Dalton, and then at Mike. "You know, she's right. I'm sorry. This whole thing is so confusing. You can't imagine how we've been harassed by the media by this thing. It's fortunate I can remember anything from that night."

"I completely understand Mr. and Mrs. Burke, and I won't trouble you any longer. I thank you for your cooperation. You've been a great help. If I may, I would like to call someone who is working with me in this matter and make sure that's all we need. I don't want to have to bother you again with more questions. Please excuse me while I make the call." And with that, he got up and walked out of the conference room.

Checking the overhead fluorescent lighting, which he believed would negate the necessity of a flash, stopping for a moment outside the door he looked back in and saw Dalton conversing with both Mr. and Mrs. Burke. He could tell that he was irritated and quickly pulled out his cell phone while he was occupied and snapped several pictures, hoping that the image might be enough to confirm his identity.

Waiting a few minutes out of sight, Mike opened the door and made a display out of shutting off his cell phone and putting it in his pocket. Moving over to Mr. and Mrs. Burke, he shook their hands and thanked them again for their cooperation, then quickly moved over to Dalton until he was very close, and without extending his hand, said, "Mr. Dalton, I'm almost certain I'll be seeing more of you. Thanks for your cooperation," and he turned and left the room.

Mike had asked the cab driver to wait outside the laboratories, and they took the same route back to the airport. Mike didn't even have to look. He knew he wasn't being followed. There was no purpose in it. During the ride to the airport, Mike sat back and thought. They're clearly lying, but why? They're both part of Hamilton Industries, and Dalton works for Hamilton Industries, and Mike had seen his type before – former military, possible mercenary, definitely a killer. There was a pattern here . . . he just had to connect the dots.

ST. THOMAS
ST. JOHN
U.S. V.I.

CHAPTER 19

Mike made his flight to St. Thomas and the 5:30 ferry from Red Hook to Cruz Bay. He walked into the Zone D station approximately one hour later. When he asked the desk Sergeant to be escorted back to Jake's cell, he was told that Jake was in an interrogation room with Commander Lucien, and Mike demanded the guard to take him there.

"Wait here," the guard said as they approached the interrogation room, and he knocked and stuck his head inside. Mike heard the response.

"By all means, let Mr. Lang come in."

Mike entered the room and looked at Jake, who said, "Commander Lucien is just here delivering more good news."

Lucien stood up and extended his hand to Mike, who shook it, never taking his eyes off Lucien's face.

"Commander Armand Lucien . . . a pleasure, Mr. Lang."

"Yeah, nice to meet you, too," said Mike.

"Unfortunately, I was just going over additional evidence we have received with Mr. Sullivan," said Lucien, "and I'm afraid it solidifies our position in this matter. Our technical staff having gone over Mr. Sullivan's computer files, we have uncovered a stream of e-mail between Mr. Sullivan and Mr. Bollinger concerning Mr. Bollinger's knowledge of Mr. Sullivan's prior criminal activity with

Benjamin Matthews, and Mr. Sullivan's admission that, in fact, he was so involved. Additionally, we have traced the serial number on the murder weapon back to its original owner, a Cuban whose family had been in the tobacco industry in the Tampa area for over a century. It was his grandfather's chiveta, which was given to Mr. Sullivan. Fortunately, he had taken a picture of the item before the presentation, and the serial number is clearly legible," said Lucien, pushing a photograph toward Jake and Mike, who was standing by him. "Additionally, here are photographs that were taken of Mr. Sullivan's office by my men, and in conversation with me, Mr. Sullivan had indicated that the chiveta that had been presented to him was on a stand on his credenza. These photos clearly show that stand is empty," and Lucien pushed over to Jake and Mike a photograph of a close up of a stand, with the chiveta clearly absent. "The forensic inspection of the blood has confirmed that the blood on Mr. Sullivan's clothes belongs to Mr. Bollinger, as do traces of blood in Mr. Sullivan's shower and sink drain.

"I'd like a copy of all the evidence you have here, Commander."

Lucien looked at him and replied, "I'm sorry, Mr. Lang. The last request for a copy of the file came from Mr. Braxton, Mr. Sullivan's attorney. He is the only person to whom we can give evidence."

"Well, I'm the investigator on the case," said Mike.

"Are you saying you are here in an official capacity on behalf of the United States Justice Department, Mr. Lang?"

Remembering his conversation with Bates and Kirkland, Mike answered, "No, I'm a private investigator hired by Mr. Sullivan in this matter."

"I'm sorry, Mr. Lang, but private investigators do not have a right of access here. If Mr. Braxton requests the information, we will be happy to give it to him, but I am sorry I cannot give it to you."

Mike looked at Jake.

"Wait," said Jake, "it gets better."

Looking back at Lucien, Mike said, "What's he talking about?"

"You must understand, Mr. Lang, that Mr. Bollinger was very popular in the islands. The people are very upset. We have been receiving threats of a very ominous nature regarding Mr. Sullivan, and we are concerned that we cannot adequately protect him at this facility. As we speak, the Chief Prosecutor of the Superior Court..."

"That would be Donaldson?" interrupted Mike.

"Yes," said Lucien. "Mr. Donaldson is presenting an emergency petition to his Honor, Emmit Denton, to have this matter certified as a capital case based upon the evidence and requesting an immediate transfer of Mr. Sullivan. He's going to be moved to a more secure facility – The Golden Grove Adult Correctional Facility – Sunday at 2:00 P.M. Tomorrow is March 31st, Transfer Day, celebrating the transfer of the Virgin Islands to the United States from Denmark in 1917, and on that day no one in the islands works. The streets will be full and we do not believe that we can establish a secure route, given the crowds, to move him tomorrow, so we will wait until Sunday."

Having put the evidence back in the evidence box, Lucien took out his handkerchief and wiped his hands, folded his handkerchief neatly, and put it back in his pocket.

"Good day, gentlemen," and with that, Lucien left.

"Mike, do you remember when I was on that panel for prison reform when we had all those damn meetings? You know the worst prison in the United States? Golden Grove. Inmate beatings, stabbings, gangs running the place. It's operating through a receivership obtained by the Department of Justice taking the local Bureau of Corrections to court in 2011. There's no way they're sending me there because it's safer."

"Why now?" asked Mike.

"Because Braxton can't get a writ of habeas corpus until Monday morning. They want to make sure I'm moved before that happens."

Mike got up and began pacing back and forth.

"Any good news from your end?" asked Jake.

Mike kept moving.

"Mike! Did you hear me?"

"Yeah, yeah, yeah. They're . . . they're lying. Their statements were probably force-fed to them by somebody. I doubt if they were even there."

"Christ Mike! That's great news! Let's get it to Arthur. It will help."

Mike stopped and stared at Jake. "Jake, you don't get it."

"What are you talking about?"

"If Braxton's going in Monday morning to get a writ of habeas corpus, that writ can get you out of Golden Grove . . ."

"I would hope so . . . so what?"

"Jake, if we let them make this transfer, by Monday morning you'll be dead. They know the federal judge is going to grant the writ. They know that'll get you off the islands. Whoever did all this isn't about to let that happen. They're sending you to Golden Grove to be killed."

The truth of what Mike was saying gradually sank in and Jake looked up. "So what do we do now?"

"I'm going to go make some calls. Then I'll be back first thing in the morning."

"You're going to make some calls?" said Jake. "That's your solution to prevent me from being killed?"

Mike turned, walked over to Jake, and smacked him on the shoulder. "Hey, take it easy. I'm good, but I'm not that good. Planning a prison break isn't easy, you know. You are leaving this place, but when you do, you're going to be with me." Mike smacked Jake on the shoulder again and said, "Now let me get to work."

Jake watched Mike leave and the door to the interrogation room close behind him. He knew Mike, and he had no doubt that soon he would be a fugitive, but at least he wouldn't be dead . . . hopefully.

CHAPTER 20

On the way back to his hotel, Mike stopped at a convenience store and picked up a prepaid cell phone. Once he got to his room, he checked the contact list from his own phone and punched in a number. After a long minute, a voice at the other end announced, "Soggy Dollar."

"Lou?"

"Who is this?"

"This is Mike Lang."

"Mike! How are you?"

"Right now I am someone who could use some help."

"This wouldn't have anything to do with your friend, would it?"

"Most definitely," said Mike.

"Listen, give me a couple minutes and I'll call you back. It's Friday night. I'm going to see if I can get someone to cover the rest of my shift."

"Lou, I'm sorry. I don't want to cause you any trouble."

"No, no. Listen, just tell me your friend didn't do it."

"He didn't. He's being framed."

"I'll call you back in a couple minutes."

Mike had met Lou Caravaggio when he had quit his job with Jake and left Havana for the islands, questioning whether the work he did was worth it or not. It had been Lou that had talked him through it and made him see the importance of what he and Jake did.

It seemed like much longer than that, but true to his word, the prepaid cell rang in less than two minutes.

"Okay, I found a quiet spot down at the beach. Now what the hell is going on?"

Mike then gave Lou the whole story, leaving out no details so he'd have a complete understanding of what was going on and what was at stake.

When he was done, Lou said, "Someone sure went out of their way to pin this on your boy. And you're absolutely right about Golden Grove. They don't plan on him coming back."

"I know," said Mike, "that's why I'm going to get him out."

"All right, brother. What can I do?"

"I need some information, I need some equipment, and I need some paperwork. Can you help me?"

"I've got sources for the information, I think I can probably handle the equipment, and I've got a guy who specializes in paperwork."

"Like I told you, they're moving him on Sunday, so I've gotta get this all together tomorrow."

Lou replied, "Same old story, brother. Short on time – long on cash."

"That's not a problem," said Mike.

"Tell me what you need," said Lou.

Mike went down the list he compiled.

"Looks like you are definitely serious," said Lou.

"Anything a problem?"

"No, I think we're good."

"You still staying at the Sand Castle?" asked Mike.

"You know the way. Up the path from the bar. First door."

"I'll be there at 8:00 o'clock tomorrow morning."

"Whoa! Early hours, my friend."

"No time to lose, Lou."

"Well then, let me get off this phone and get to work . . . get some of my friends out of bed and see what we can do."

"Thanks, Lou. I appreciate it."

"No problem. Like I told you the last time we talked, good guys gotta fight the monsters. See you in the morning." And with that, he was gone.

Mike sat down on his bed and hoped that Lou could come through. If all went as he planned, Jake would be safe, at least temporarily, and then things would change. Then they'd begin the hunt to find the real killer who framed him.

The next call Mike made was to Eva.

"Hey Mike . . . you okay?"

"I'm fine, Eva."

"And how's Jake? How's he holding up?"

"Under the circumstances, pretty well. How's things on your end?"

"I went through all the files. The only connection I could find that Jake had to those islands was with that pretty little girl that got killed by that bastard Ortiz."

"What was her name?" asked Mike.

"Alaina Alvarez," came the reply.

"Yeah, that was the case that almost ruined Jake and brought about the whole affair with Matthews," mused Mike.

"But here's the thing, hon, I looked up everything about her, including her obituary, and other than her mother and father, it said she had no other living relatives, and the obituary said her father was some kind of an artist and her mother was a teacher. Not the kind of people able to run the type of operation you're describing."

"True," said Mike, "and not only that … Jake got the killer. Hell, he killed Ortiz himself and eventually we took care of Matthews, so we certainly got justice for that young girl. No, that can't be it. There has to be something else."

"I'll keep digging, but that's the only connection I've come up with so far," said Eva.

"All right, listen Eva, tomorrow the shit's going to hit the fan. I can't tell you why because I don't want to implicate you, but you're not going to be able to reach me. If I need anything, I'll call you."

"Mike, what's going on? What are you up to?"

"Eva, I just told you … I can't say. I'm doing everything I can to take care of Jake. Let's just leave it at that."

"All right darlin' … you boys be careful. That's all I ask."

"Understood. I'll be in touch."

Now came the final call he had to make.

"Jason, it's Mike. Am I interrupting anything?"

"Mike," said Jason Bates, "I work for the President of the United States. It doesn't matter when you call – you're always interrupting something."

"Any information you can send my way?" asked Mike.

"No. Everything seems to be as good as we can expect right now. I understand the federal courts are going to take over the matter on Monday morning and Jake will be returned to Miami, where he'll be safe, and we can try and figure out who's behind this."

"I think you need to be caught up on things, Jason."

"Such as what?"

"Did you ever hear of a prison down here called Golden Grove?"

"Unfortunately, I have. It's one of the worst. It's operating under a federal receivership."

"Yeah, well Jake is going to be transferred there on Sunday."

"What?" said Bates.

"You heard me. And I think the real purpose of the transfer is so that he doesn't come back."

"You're suggesting that the local courts and police are trying to have Jake killed?"

"It's like I told Jake, Jason, Monday morning, if Art Braxton comes through, Jake leaves these islands. Whoever set this up does not want that to happen."

"I just talked to Braxton today," said Bates. "He didn't mention anything about a transfer. I don't even know if he knows about it."

"There was an emergency petition being presented to the local court today to effectuate a transfer on Sunday, and Braxton can't have his petition heard until Monday," said Mike.

"I don't know what to tell you, Mike. I don't have any other information. I'll try and get hold of Arthur and see if there's something we can do."

"I just called to let you know one thing, Jason."

"Which is?"

"I'm not going to let Jake go to that prison . . . I'm not going to let him get killed."

"Mike, if you remember, Lester and I gave you certain parameters within which you had to operate."

"To hell with your parameters, Jason. Things have changed here on the ground, and I didn't call you to waste your time talking about your parameters. I called you as a courtesy. This is the last time we'll probably talk for a while. I just wanted you to know . . . I'm going to do what I have to do."

"Mike, listen . . ."

And with that, Mike hung up the phone.

Mike had just stretched out on the bed, thinking to himself that he had to get some rest because tomorrow was going to be a very long day, when there was a knock on the door.

"Son of a bitch!" said Mike, as he opened the door and Bill Adams walked into his room. "Bill Adams . . . how the hell are you?"

"Better than you, my friend . . . better than you."

"Tell me about it," said Mike. "To what do I owe the honor of this visit?"

"Let's just say your presence is being felt on the islands."

"Bill, we've known each other a long time. Did you come here to put a leash on me?"

"Do I have to?"

"Do you really want to know?"

"Mike, come on. I'm Special Agent in Charge down here. The Director found out about Golden Grove and sent me here to find you. He had some concern for some reason that you won't wait until Monday."

"He probably just got a call from Bates," said Mike. "I was just on the phone with him."

"I think the call actually came from Kirkland," said Adams, "but I think the message was from Bates. I am to request from you, as your friend and old comrade, that you do nothing illegal or, I believe the word was, 'foolhardy.'"

Mike got up to walk around the room, came back to where Bill was sitting on one of the chairs, and stood in front of him.

"Bill, you know if they send him to Garden Grove, he's not coming back."

Adams looked at the floor and then back up at Mike. "I'd have to say the odds are against it."

"You've known me for a long time, Bill. You think I'll let that happen?"

Adams got up and moved towards the door. "Mike, I came here officially to give you the position of the Director of the FBI, as well as probably the Justice Department of the United States, and the President. Unofficially, I know exactly what you're going to do. Officially, when you do it, I'm going to have to come after you. Unofficially . . ." and he walked over to the desk again, picked up a pen and paper, and wrote something down. "That's a private number that not too many people know about. If you get yourself in a jam, call it. If I can help you, I will."

"I can't ask for more than that," said Mike.

"I've said it before and I'll say it again . . . you were always a pain in the ass. Just be careful."

"Thanks, Bill."

After Adams left, Mike sat on the bed and punched the number he had been given into his phone, ripped the piece of paper into tiny shreds, and flushed it down the toilet. He went back to lay on the bed, even though he knew there would probably be no sleep this night.

JOST VAN DYKE

B.V.I.

CHAPTER 21

After a fitful night with very little sleep, Mike rose, showered, and was at Jake's cell by 6:00 A.M.

"I take it you couldn't sleep either," said Jake.

"Too much going on." Moving close to Jake, Mike said, "Listen, here's how this is gonna work," and he went over his phone call with Lou the night before, what he was going to do the remainder of the day, and what would happen on Sunday.

Jake walked away, thinking, and turned. "Hell of a plan. Think it'll work?"

"Has to . . . it's our only shot."

"Hey, we've come up with worse. Let's do it."

"Go over by that wall," said Mike, taking off the floral shirt he was wearing. "Put this on." Mike then took off the sunglasses that were resting on top of his head and popped out the lenses. "Put these on. They'll look like clear glasses. Straighten up your hair a little, but not too much. Okay, hold still." And with that, Mike pulled his cell phone out of his pocket and took several pictures of Jake standing with his back against the wall.

"All right, listen, try to eat well today and get some rest. Things are going to move fast tomorrow." Mike started out of the cell and then turned. "Oh, and by the way . . . if I don't show up Sunday morning, everything went to hell, but I'll probably meet you at Golden Grove."

"Really?" said Jake. "That's what you're gonna leave me with?"

Mike turned and smiled. "Just think how happy you'll be when I show up."

After leaving the zone station, Mike made his way to Ocean Runner Power Boat Rental in Cruz Bay and, after showing his U.S. Sailing Certification, rented a 25-foot Mako power boat with twin Evenrude E-Tech motors using a passport and credit card naming him as one Michael Warden. Soon Mike was headed out past Lind Point and passed through the Windward Passage off the western edge of Great Thatch Island as he passed into British territory and headed into the mooring area in White Bay on Jost Van Dyke.

Going over the side and landing up to his knees in the shallow water, he made his way to the beach, up past the Soggy Dollar Bar, onto the path heading to the Sandcastle Hotel. He arrived at the first door and knocked.

"Who's there?" came a voice from inside.

"Mike Lang."

The door opened, and there stood Lou Caravaggio, T-shirt and shorts, as usual. The only change from their last encounter being the Glock 17 he held at his side. Mike looked at the gun and then back to Lou.

"Hey, this is like a black ops. You can't be too careful, my friend. Come in." Extending his hand, he said, "Nice to see you again, brother. Sorry for the circumstances. How's your friend holding up?"

"Best as he can. He'll be better this time tomorrow."

"Hope so. Want to go over your inventory?"

"Yeah, let me see what you got."

On the bed was an array of weaponry, electronics, and file folders. Lou reached for the file folders first.

"Here's everything I could get you on Bollinger. Ran some financials on your other request. Some interesting stuff in there. And this is the info on the company. Waiting for a friend of mine at MI6 to give me the info on our security expert. From what I got preliminarily, he's the real deal, but my guy is going to need a photo to confirm."

"Then we'll get him one," said Mike.

"What about the Burkes?"

Lou picked up another folder. "Short version: Mr. and Mrs. Burke are an average couple, except their four year old daughter has Cystic Fibrosis. A week or so ago she was taken to the St. Louis Children's Hospital for a potential lung transplant. Burke's brother lives there, and that hospital is world-renowned for their work with children with that disease." Lou looked up at Mike. "I know there are a lot of programs out there to help with that sort of thing, but I'm thinking a lot of cash for treatment like that. The Burke family doesn't take in that kind of money."

"Lou, if you were given that choice – to lie to get that kind of treatment for your child – what would you do?"

"Point taken, brother."

"What about Hamilton Industries?" said Mike.

"Crazy stuff going on here. Evidently, Hamilton's been making a lot of political and economic connections with Venezuela and Mexico. His lab specializes in developing technology for oil and gas exploration and extraction, and he was the guy that supported Donaldson in the recent election. My guy found a rumor that he was attempting to buy the old oil refinery, which leads me to Bollinger. You know a lot of stuff about him already, but when my source checked the court records, he found that Bollinger, under a company name, had filed an injunction in federal court to stop Hamilton Industries' purchase of the refinery and request that the whole matter be removed to federal jurisdiction because there can be no fair trial in the judiciary on the island. And get this, the hearing was going to be this Monday."

"Sounds like a good reason for murder," said Mike. "What about our Zone Commander?"

"I told you, the financials were interesting. Hard to trace, but my guy is good. Lucien's dirty. They reveal he's been getting money in certain increments for years now. Just haven't been able to tag the source yet."

"So we've got the Burkes working for Hamilton Industries, who need money to save their daughter's life, and they're the key witnesses against Jake concerning this murder; we have Bollinger trying to stop Hamilton Industries from buying a refinery; and Hamilton has been getting cozy with Mexico and Venezuela and developing technology concerning oil and gas. So how about this," said Mike as he turned and looked at Lou, "Hamilton, through his mercenary Dalton, kills Bollinger and closes out the legal proceedings, needs the refinery for whatever he's doing with Mexico and Venezuela with oil and gas – big money – again, good reason to get Bollinger out of the way; the Burkes were coerced into testifying against Jake because of their daughter's medical condition."

"Sounds like you got something, Mike," said Lou.

"Yeah, but here's what's missing . . . why Jake? Why pin it on him? Who is this guy Hamilton? Did you find any tie-in?"

"Nothing," said Lou. "The guy inherited the company from his father, Alexander Hamilton, and yeah, there is a connection to the Alexander Hamilton, has tons of money, lives on an estate up in the hills, he's a widower, and his only daughter died a couple years ago. Can't find any business ties to Miami, no legal proceedings in Miami, nothing to tie him to Jake."

"There has to be some connection, Lou, there just has to be. They didn't just pick him out of the blue for no reason, and when we find out what that connection is, we'll prove who's behind all this."

"All right," said Mike, heading toward the bed, "let's look at the rest of this stuff."

"What else do you have for me?"

"Here's the electronic gear you wanted. Half a dozen burner phones, no GPS. Flag pin – really a camera, visuals show up in these glasses, remote feed to this laptop. Again, no GPS."

"And this?" asked Mike.

"This ring's a receiver. Can pick up any conversation, range of up to 200 yards, tied into the same computer. Two Glocks, multiple clips, serial numbers filed off, untraceable. Taser and zip ties."

"How about the other thing?"

"Right over here. Syringe already loaded." Lou Caravaggio opened up a case. Inside was a syringe and what appeared to be a time-release capsule, along with what looked like a wrist watch. "I gotta tell you Mike, this is beautiful. Syringe fully loaded, constant GPS, no limitation. As far as the distance these islands cover, we're good. Pick up the tracking on the watch."

"And what's the capsule?"

"That's the sugar pill."

Mike looked around. "You did great, Lou! What's the tariff?"

"Mike, you know, some of this stuff is really state of the art."

"Hey, Lou, I'm not here to dicker with you. What'd it cost?"

"Twenty large."

Mike had removed the money from the ceiling tile and packed up his belongings and had checked out from the hotel in Cruz Bay, knowing he wouldn't be back. Opening his duffle bag, he took out the cash and put down two packages of $10,000 each.

"What about the paper?"

"You've gotta go see the guy."

"And who's the guy and where do I find him?"

"Willie T's in the Bight off Norman Island. The Greek. Here's the coordinates. Put 'em in your GPS and it'll take you right to it."

"He gonna have everything ready?"

"When you sent me the photos last night, I sent them to him."

"He said he could handle all the rest?"

"Everything should be ready by noon today."

Mike began loading all the gear into his duffle bag. "Well, that gives me some time."

"I got you guys a room under an assumed name right next door. Let's move your stuff in."

"Great Lou. Hope it wasn't too much of a problem for you."

"Nah, the owner owes me. We're good. I do have a favor to ask though."

"What do you need?" asked Mike.

"I'd like to come along on this one."

Mike stopped what he was doing, turned back from the bed, and looked at Lou. "I can't ask you to do that. I've got a feeling of who we're dealing with, but I'm not sure. I know whoever it is has some clout. You don't want to get involved in this."

"Look, you're not asking. I'm offering. And I do want to get involved. Tending bar, serving drinks to all those lovely young things is great, but you know what, every once in while I get an itch for the former life. You know what I mean? Besides, you and Jake are the good guys. I want to help."

"What about your job?"

"I have vacation time."

"You can leave? Just like that?"

"Let's just say I've done some work for the boss. He and I have a certain relationship. I'll tell him a friend of mine is coming to stay for a little while. I'm good."

"You sure?" said Mike.

"I told you . . . I'm in."

"Okay, here's the plan."

When he was done explaining his plan to free Jake, Mike walked over and extended his hand and he and Lou shook. "Don't say I didn't warn you."

"Don't worry, brother. It'll be fun," Lou said, smiling broadly.

"All right, I'm good to go."

"All right Mike. Follow me next door. We'll get you situated before you take off."

Between the two of them, it only took one trip to unload the boat and move Mike's gear into the room next to Lou. Looking around at the room with two single beds, small desk, and the now standard flat-screen TV, Mike looked at Lou and said, "Not a bad way to live."

"What the hell. I enjoy it."

"All right," said Mike, "it's time for me to get to Norman Island."

"I'll walk down to the beach with you," said Lou.

It was a beautiful day in paradise. Mike looked out over the sparkling blue water, the boats moored, the bar already filling up, and the palm trees blowing lazily in the breeze. He turned and looked at Lou.

"You know, I am gonna come here when I have no problems and actually enjoy this place."

"Amen, brother," said Lou.

"Good luck. I'll see you in Cruz Bay," said Mike.

And with that, Mike made his way out to his rental and headed out to open water.

NORMAN ISLAND

B.V.I.

CHAPTER 22

Mike entered the coordinates Lou had given him into the GPS and headed to Norman Island, famous for being thought by many as the basis for Robert Lewis Stevenson's Treasure Island, for the Caves the water had eroded into Treasure Point, and the Willie T.

The Willie T was a floating restaurant and bar that sat in the Bight off Norman Island. Formerly a wooden Baltic trading vessel, it was ultimately replaced with a steel, hundred-foot schooner. It was named for one William Thornton, who was born on Jost Van Dyke, educated in Scotland as a physician, but won immortality as the architect of the United States Capitol building.

Mike made his way, again past Great Thatch Island, through the Narrows, around East End Point of St. John, and took a course dead center between Flannigan Island and a rock formation known as The Indians, across Flannigan Passage, and headed into the Bight, cutting the motor and drifting in to tie up to the Willie T. Climbing to the afterdeck, as Lou had instructed, he found the Greek sitting under a canopy. Looking around, he saw that there were already young boaters drinking shots from the water ski, and others, already having had their shots, jumping off the rear railing into the Bight. He approached the bespectacled gentleman who was reading a book, with salt and pepper hair, linen slacks, and a silk shirt, who did not lift his head from the book as Mike sat down. Mike waited for the Greek to speak.

"Sorry. Mr. Lang, I presume?" said the Greek. "Interesting work on ancient Peruvian architecture. Wanted to finish the chapter."

The accent was definitely British, and the pale skin and facial structure didn't seem Greek to Mike.

"And you're the Greek, I presume?"

"Ah, yes – the nickname. You see, Mr. Lang, I was actually a visiting professor from Oxford University on loan to the University of Athens, lecturing on ancient writings. I always had a fondness for documents, papers, that sort of thing. And unfortunately I was in that position when the nastiness broke out in Cypress and I was recruited by some people in my government to assist those who might have to flee. I became quite adept at it, and eventually, gained some renown . . . not always among the most proper circles . . . and soon, the very government which had recruited me was trying to imprison me, and I decided it was time to seek a new venue for my work. And here I am."

"So you chose to come here . . . British territory . . . as your base of operations?"

The Greek laughed as another somewhat intoxicated young lady dove of the back of the Willie T.

"You see, my friend, time goes on, alliances change, and those who are our friends become our enemies, and those who are enemies become our friends."

Mike looked at him long and hard. "You're back working for MI6."

The Green shrugged his shoulders. "At times, my talents are needed, or some piece of information is required."

Mike's jaw stiffened and he leaned forward. "Can I assume that our business will remain private?"

The Greek leaned back, his deep-set dark eyes squinting in the sun. "I do not believe your friend to be a murderer, but whatever this situation is, it is one for the Americans to resolve. I have had no inquiries, nor do I believe I will . . . and we have a business arrangement to conclude." And with that, he handed Mike a manila envelope. Mike opened it and looked inside.

"Excellent work."

"I try my best," said the Greek. "You have to realize it was on short notice."

"I understand, and I presume that will enter into the price."

The Greek shrugged his shoulders and smiled. "The cost of doing business, shall we say?"

"And what is the cost?" asked Mike.

"For the documents . . . ten thousand. The cost for the two men you wanted and their expenses . . . an additional three thousand each. Sixteen thousand dollars."

Mike looked around to make sure they were not being observed, reached in his duffle bag, which he had swung over his shoulder when he left the boat, and handed the Greek two packets wrapped in paper.

"There's ten thousand in each one. The four thousand is a bonus."

"May I ask for what?" said the Greek.

"Other men will come and question you. I would prefer they receive no answers. Let's say they may try various means of persuasion."

"Ah," said the Greek, "I see."

The Green reached into his linen jacket, placing one packet in the inside left pocket and the other in the inside right pocket.

"Mr. Lang, I am afraid I will be forced to speak regardless of your generous offer. I will have to tell whoever asks me, after some coercion, of course, that I have prepared two sets of documents for a man meeting your description who came to me. Those documents included airline tickets to Miami in the United States, and so far as I know, the two men in question have left the island. And I apologize in advance for not keeping my silence about these issues, but my physical strengths are somewhat diminished and, unfortunately, I can only be brave for so long." And with that, he smiled.

Mike smiled back and extended his hand. "A pleasure doing business with you."

"Likewise," said the Greek. "May we conclude our negotiations with a drink?"

"Perhaps later, under better circumstances. But now, unfortunately, I have further business to conduct."

"I understand. God's speed, Mr. Lang."

Mike nodded, turned, and walked away, passing another group of revelers hoisting the water ski, happily toasting the fact that they were young and in the warm waters of the Caribbean without a care in the world.

ST. JOHN

U.S. V.I.

CHAPTER 23

The sky was an azure blue and the water was crystal clear as Mike made his way out of the Bight and across the Flannigan Passage. He headed for Ram Head, the southern-most point of St. John, and stayed close to the southern coast as he made his way to Cruz Bay. After finding a berth to tie up the boat, he made his way to the Zone Station. The streets had been crowded, full of revelers celebrating Transfer Day. Mike had made the right decision. If the only person in the station was the desk sergeant and everyone else was out mingling with the crowd, it would be easier to slip away through all the people, even though it was not yet dark.

Mike approached the door to the station and punched a number into his cell phone.

"Are you in position?"

"Ready to go."

"All right, on my mark. Go. Five minutes."

Entering the station, Mike approached the desk sergeant and asked to see Jake. He heard no other voices and saw no other personnel as he was taken back to Jake's cell. After opening the cell door, the sergeant left them alone and returned to his station.

As Mike entered the cell, Jake asked, "So what's going on?"

Mike continued to stare at his watch. "Just a minute."

"Mike, what are you doing?"

Mike held up his hand. "It's all part of the plan."

"What plan?" asked Jake.

"Now." Mike started screaming, "Help! Help! Help! Get me outta here! Help!"

The desk sergeant, hearing Mike's cries, came running back, unaware that Lou Caravaggio was right behind him, and before he realized his mistake, Lou used the taser on him and put him to the ground. Mike and Lou then bound him with plastic zip ties and put a gag in his mouth.

Opening the backpack that Lou had carried into the station, Mike looked up from it and said, "Sorry Jake. Lou Caravaggio . . . Lou, Jake Sullivan."

Lou took the time to extend his hand. "A pleasure."

"Me, too," said Jake, somewhat bewildered.

"We'll do complete introductions later," said Mike. "Right now, we don't have time. Let's move," he said as he took out a Glock from the bag and handed it to Jake, as well as identity papers showing Jake to be one Jacob Green from Tampa, Florida. The papers that Mike was now carrying showed him to be one Michael Thompson from Sarasota, Florida.

"Why use our same first names?" said Jake. "Won't that give somebody a hint as to who we are?"

"No. That's something I learned in the FBI. When someone calls you by your first name, your tendency, when the adrenaline is rushing, is to turn and respond in some fashion. This way, if that happens, it still goes along with the new identities."

They also took out a change of clothes and a baseball cap for Jake and he quickly changed, discarding the clothes he had on for several days.

"All right, follow and stay close," said Mike to Jake. "If we get separated, we meet at the boat docks."

"I'll meet you at Sandcastle," said Lou, heading off in a direction opposite to what Jake and Mike would take.

Weaving their way through the crowd, Jake and Mike only passed police on two separate occasions.

"Just keep your head up," said Mike. "Look natural," and they passed both points without incident. Mike noticed Jake's expression and said, "Don't' look so glum . . . you're a free man."

"Yeah, I know . . . but now I'm a fugitive. Each time we passed those guys I thought I was going to hear, 'Hey you! Stop!'"

"Yeah, but they didn't Jake. So far, we've pulled this off, and you're looking at this the wrong way. You're not a fugitive. You're a federal prosecutor working a case. You're trying to solve a murder, and that's what you need to focus on, cause that's the only way you're going to get out of this."

Mike led Jake to the slip where the motor boat he had rented was moored. Soon they were exiting Cruz Bay and turned northeast through the Windward Passage and on to Jost Van Dyke. Hopefully, Lou was already there, waiting for them.

As they approached White Bay, Mike looked at Jake, who had ridden so far in silence, and said, "All right Jake. This is going to be home for a while. This is where we start taking back your life."

JOST VAN DYKE

BV.I.

CHAPTER 24

Mike lowered the anchor at one of the off-shore mooring points and he and Jake went over the side, making their way through the water to the beach.

"Jake, welcome to the Soggy Dollar Bar," said Mike, pointing to his right as they made their way up to the Sandcastle.

"Okay, you going to tell me who this Lou guy is?" said Jake.

Mike stopped and turned. "Yeah, he's a bartender here."

"A bartender?" said Jake.

"Well, he's a little bit more than a bartender. Former Navy Seal, black ops specialist, seems to know everybody in these islands, and so far, he's been able to get anything done I've asked him to do, and most importantly Jake . . . he volunteered to help us." Mike turned and started moving again.

"How'd you meet this guy?" said Jake.

Mike said over his shoulder, "This is where I came after Paula died. He helped me through it. I should really hate him. He made me come back to work with you."

"Sounds like a first-rate, stand-up guy to me," said Jake as they approached Lou's door.

After one knock on the door, it opened, and Lou looked out, Glock in his right hand by his side, and motioned them to come in.

"Have a seat guys . . . chair, bed, whatever. I just talked to one of my contacts on St. John. No alarm has been sounded yet, so either they haven't found the desk sergeant, or they don't want to make public what's happened. Either way, I figure we have some time."

"Good," said Mike, taking a seat on the bed. "Let's figure out where we go from here. And I guess we better start by bringing Jake up to speed."

As Lou sat down, Jake got up from the chair where he had sat and extended his hand.

"I understand you volunteered your services."

"Pleased to help, Jake."

"I want you to know I appreciate it."

"No problem, man. No problem."

"All right, so what do we have?" said Jake.

And Lou and Mike proceeded to go over all the files and information they had gathered. When they were done, Jake sat and thought about it.

"It has to be Hamilton," he said. "He has the resources, he has the motive, and he has the means with this Dalton, or whoever he is."

"Jake, can you think of any tie-in you'd have with this guy? Any of his businesses? Anything you did that would make him want to go after you?"

"I know I've never had any dealings with him, Mike. I've had no cases involving his companies, and I know I've never met him. Like I told you before, and like Eva confirmed, the only contact I've had on these islands has been Alaina. I know her parents were hurt, and rightfully so when the case against Ortiz got tossed out, but I'm sure they know what happened with Ortiz and Matthews."

"Yeah," said Lou, "it was all over the news down here like it was everywhere else."

"And they were simple people," said Jake. "I think the father was some type of an artist, and the mother was a school teacher like Eva said. And the obituary said there were no other relatives. They couldn't fund an operation like this. How would they make contact with a guy like Dalton? It just doesn't make sense."

Mike got up and started pacing. "There has to be some connection Jake. They targeted you for a reason, and it can't just be your relationship with Fletcher. They've taken a big chance here. Like it or not, as much as I hate to admit it, you're a public figure. You know how these things usually work. They get somebody unknown, somebody who's in and out, to kill a guy like Bollinger – not a semi-celebrity. Besides, they didn't just want to get rid of you Jake . . . they want to destroy you. They want to destroy your image . . . your reputation . . . before they have you die. Otherwise, they would have just killed you. This whole frame-up of trying to tie you into Matthews is a way to destroy everything you stand for."

"Mike, I know you're right, but I can't figure out what the tie-in is. I can't figure out who's behind it, or for what reason, but I'll tell you this . . . I'm done sitting back waiting for things to happen. To hell with them. Let's go after them."

"That's what I like to hear," said Lou, "let's go get these bastards!"

"It would be a hell of a lot easier to go after them if we know who they are," said Mike. "Let me make a couple calls to see if there's anything new."

Mike took out one of the burner phones and showed it to Jake and Lou.

"Look, we're going to have these phones with us. If you need one, use one. I have a couple numbers already set in here. One is Eva's, one is Bates, another one is a number Bill Adams gave me."

"Adams?" said Jake, "with the FBI?"

"Yeah. He came to see me last night."

"And?" said Jake.

"I think he knew what was going to happen, and officially, he's going to come after us."

"Well, that's just great!" said Jake.

"But unofficially, he'll help us if he can."

Jake looked long and hard at Mike. "You trust him?"

"I do," said Mike.

"Good enough for me. Lou?"

"Yeah, me too."

Mike then punched in the number for Eva and waited while it rang. "Eva? Mike. Yeah, we're good. I have Jake and he's safe. Anything on the news up there yet? Alright, listen, there's something you have to do. There's two guys coming in to the airport later this afternoon. Here's their names and flight information. I want you to pick them up, find a non-descript motel somewhere, and put them in there for three nights. Make sure they talk to no one and do nothing to draw attention to themselves. Tell them if they handle themselves right, there'll be a bonus for them when the three days are up."

"You going to tell me what all this is about?"

"Yeah. I just broke Jake out of jail. Those guys are supposed to be us fleeing the island and heading for Miami."

"You busted Jake out of jail?" asked Eva.

"Yeah, it was the only way to save his sorry ass, Eva. I had to do it."

"Is he all right?" said Eva. "Let me talk to him."

"Here Jake. Say hello."

"Eva, I'm okay. I'm all right. Just do what Mike's telling you to do. Everything is going to be fine."

"How'd you get yourself into this mess?" said Eva.

"That's what we're trying to figure out Eva," said Jake. "Just don't worry. Everything's okay. We'll call you if we need anything else, all right? Oh . . . Eva, anything more on Alaina Alvarez?"

"Nothing more than I told Mike," said Eva. "I can't find anything else out about her."

"All right. Thanks Eva, and take care. With any luck, we'll see you soon!"

"Please Jake. You and Mike take care of yourselves."

"We will. Gotta go." And with that, Jake hung up, looked at Mike, and shook his head. "Same old Eva."

Mike smiled. "She is the best, isn't she? All right," said Mike. "Now the call I don't want to make."

"Bates?" asked Jake.

"Yeah. Gotta give him the bad news. My not stepping on any toes down here has come to an end."

"As if it ever started," said Lou.

Surprisingly, the phone was answered by a woman. "Jason Bates? Who shall I say is calling?"

"Is he there? Could you just put him on the line?"

"Hold on, please."

Mike looked at Jake with a quizzical expression.

"I'm sorry, evidently Mr. Bates knows who you are, and he told me to give you a message. Make sure you take care of the package in your possession, and do everything possible to provide him with the data he needs so that he can take possession of the package free and clear of all liens and encumbrances."

"That's it?" said Mike, "and he doesn't want to talk to me?"

"That was the message, sir."

"All right. Let him know . . ." and before Mike could finish, the line went dead.

"Bates has efficient help, too," said Mike.

"What's going on?" said Jake.

"He gave me a coded message about taking care of the package – which is you – getting him the data he needs – which is proof of what the hell is going on – so that he could take possession of the package – you again – without any liens or encumbrances – meaning he wants this over before he raises a finger."

"I have an idea," said Jake. "I don't know if it will work, but I think it's worth a try."

"I'm all ears," said Mike.

"Let's go to St. Croix. Let's take this straight to Hamilton Industries. Let's arrange a meeting with this Adolphus Hamilton, and let's let him know that we know what's going on. We need to flip this thing. They need to know we're not going to sit back and wait for them to come after us, but that we're going to go after them."

Mike thought it over. "Might work, or . . . get us killed."

"You know what else we need to do while we're there?" said Jake. "We need to get the Burkes off by themselves. I think they're in a situation they don't want to be in, and they have to start figuring sooner or later that they're expendable . . . they're a loose end . . . and they might just be willing to come to our side. Lou?"

"Sounds like a plan to me. Let's go."

"Lou," said Jake, "you said you had some preliminary information on this guy Dalton. Anything else?"

"The preliminary information won't do us much good, Jake. It's just that this guy shows up a couple months ago, no past, no one knows how he entered the islands, and all of a sudden he's head of security for Hamilton Industries. He doesn't exist on paper, but my guy at MI6 says that if we can get him a photo, he might be able to track him through Interpol and find out who he is. Mike got a cell phone picture of him while he was talking to the Burkes. It might be enough for my guy to do his thing."

"Let me see the picture," said Jake to Mike.

Mike took out his cell phone and pulled up the picture and handed it over.

"Jesus Christ!" said Jake.

"What?" said Mike.

"He's the Goddamned bartender!"

"You sure?" asked Mike.

"Absolutely. I won't forget that son of a bitch!"

"No question now," said Lou, "Hamilton's our boy. But before we see him, I think we need to find out who this guy is."

"What do we need to do?" asked Mike.

"My contact operates out of Road Town on Tortola. Let me make some calls and see how he wants to handle it."

And with that, Lou grabbed a phone and walked outside. Fifteen minutes later he was back through the door.

"It's set up. He wants me to meet him in person. We're going to do it at Soper's Hole at West End, closest point to us. More laid-back and touristy. Easy for us to make our connection. Problem is, he's on something right now and can't do it until tomorrow. However, I have an alternative plan until then."

"Which is?" asked Mike.

Everybody gets a good shower, good shave, and a little sleep. Tonight – my treat. We go to Foxy's over at Great Harbor, have ourselves a delicious meal, a few drinks, and tomorrow, bright eyed and bushy tailed, we take it to these sons-a-bitches."

Mike looked at Jake. "Best plan I've heard so far. Lou, you're on," said Mike.

That evening, the three of them, bathed, groomed, and rested, made their way to Foxy's – one of the legendary bars in the Caribbean – and moored their boat in Great Harbor. Something new had been added to Jake's wardrobe – a bandage on his left arm, which he rubbed as he sat down.

"That thing still hurt?" asked Lou.

"Damn right it hurts," said Jake.

"Come on," said Mike, "it's just a little knife point."

"You want to have this thing put in your arm?" asked Jake.

Lou shook his head. "Hey, Jake, it's going to hurt a lot more if someone tries to take it out."

"Any problems with the injection?" said Mike.

Jake rubbed his neck. "No, doesn't seem to be."

"Well then, you're all set," said Mike.

"Thanks," said Jake. "I appreciate it."

After his shower, Mike had opened a small incision on Jake's left arm and pushed in what Lou had referred to as the sugar pill . . . the placebo . . . the phony tracking device that someone like Dalton would surely notice. After cleaning the wound with alcohol, much to Jake's dismay, Mike bandaged his arm, making sure it was noticeable. Then the real tracking device, microscopic in size, was injected at the base of Jake's neck just above the shoulder, his natural height aiding in the transmission of the signal.

Philicianno "Foxy" Callwood was more a legend than the bar. Although he was getting on in years, this "troubadour-poet-entertainer-restauranteur-scallywag" still appeared occasionally to sing his insulting but beloved songs to his guests and extend a hearty handshake and smile to everyone. And if he didn't show up, there was always his life-sized mannequin, known as "Epoxy Foxy" to oversee the festivities.

Given that it was Saturday night, the "Grillzebo" was fired up and barbeque was the meal of the evening.

They agreed to share a huge platter of fresh shallots, fruits and vegetables, barbeque chicken, ribs, and mahi-mahi. Lou and Mike opted for one of the micro brews and Jake ordered a diet soda.

It was a good night – a break – especially for Jake, from what he had endured the past few days. The happiness of the crowd and their own comradery and tales from Lou strengthened the bond among them and made them ready for what was ahead. Of course, nothing compared to when the inimitable Foxy made his appearance. The crowd went wild as Foxy waved to one and all. Lou stood up and waved and caught Foxy's eye, and he started making his way over to their table.

"Don't tell me," said Mike. "He's another one of your 'guys'?"

"Can't be in these islands very long and not make friends with Foxy," said Lou.

Foxy made his way over and reached out for Lou's hand. "Lou Caravaggio! Bartender extraordinaire! Why don't you quit that place and come work for me?"

"Appreciate the offer, Foxy, as always, but it's a little more quiet over there. Suits my style."

"I understand, my man. I understand. And who might these two be?"

"Friends of mine," said Lou, "Mike and Jake."

"Well, Mike and Jake . . . welcome to Foxy's. How was the food?"

"Out of this world," said Mike.

"Agreed," said Jake.

"You watch this guy," said Foxy, pointing to Lou. "He'll get you into trouble. Catch you later Lou. Gotta see my fans."

"Take care Foxy," said Lou, and he sat back down. Lou laughed. "How about that? He thinks I'm getting you guys into trouble?"

TORTOLA

B.V.I.

CHAPTER 25

They left White Bay early Sunday morning and Lou Caravaggio steered the motor boat through open water, pulling into Soper's Hole at West End, Island of Tortola, British Virgin Islands.

Prior to casting off from Jost Van Dyke, Lou had made a phone call to his contact at MI6 and they had arranged a meeting at Pusser's Landing. Lou directed Jake and Mike to Pusser's Bar and Restaurant while he went to the Customs dock directly across from it, taking Jake and Mike's new passports with him. After several minutes, he joined them at the bar and told them that everything had gone fine, explaining that he often came to the West End and didn't expect to be questioned too thoroughly about his passengers. His familiarity proved to be true when the bartender came up and said, "Hi Lou! How are you? Haven't seen you for a while."

When the bartender asked what they would be having, Lou quickly said, "Three cups of Nelson's Blood."

Jake and Mike looked at him.

"Don't get excited boys. It's only rum. Seems you two need a history lesson. Pusser is Royal Navy slang for purser – ship's supply officer – meaning that the rum sold by this company is the same as if it came from the Royal Navy itself."

The bartender came back and set down three metal cups of rum on the bar.

"See the seamen on the mug? The flags around the top? That depicts Lord Admiral Horatio Nelson's victory at the Battle of Trafalgar in 1805. Before the battle started, Nelson had those flags flown from the top mast of his flagship HMS Victory before the battle began."

"I've read about this," said Jake. "The flags spell out 'England Expects That Every Man Will Do His Duty,' right?"

"Absolutely," said Lou. "One of the greatest sea battles of all time. Turned the tide of the Napoleonic Wars and gave England complete command of the seas for a century and a half, until we took over. Nelson was killed during the battle and his body was put in a keg of rum for the trip home. That's the term – Nelson's Blood – for Royal Navy rum. So with that, a toast . . . to great victories of the underdog!"

"You trying to tell us something, Lou?" said Mike as the three banged their mugs and Lou and Mike took a drink.

Just then, a man with a ball cap pulled low and a linen shirt and shorts sat down two seats away from Jake at the bar and sat a newspaper on top of the bar. The man in the ball cap ordered a drink with an umbrella, sat at the bar for a while and drank half of it, and then headed off toward the dock, leaving the newspaper behind.

Lou got up, moved around Jake and Mike, picked up the newspaper, and set it down by him.

Mike said, "That was your agent? Did he make the drop?"

Opening up the newspaper they found a dossier with a photograph. Mike said, "That's the guy who was there with Burkes."

Jake looked at the photograph. "More importantly . . . that is definitely the bartender!"

"We weren't wrong gentlemen. This is one tough son of a bitch. Real name: Aiden Vaughan. Welsh by birth and a former sergeant-major in the Royal Welsh Fusiliers. Seems like he was a good soldier up until the wars in the Balkans. He was one of thirty-three men taken captive by the Bosnian Serbs at Goraźde in 1995. Reports at the time were that all the men were eventually safely rescued, when in point of fact, Vaughan went missing. Since then, there have been reports of him turning up as a mercenary all over the globe, but no one has been able to confirm his identity or capture him. His specialty is political assassination, along with other assorted types of murder and mayhem."

While sitting at the bar, the three noticed an officer of the Royal Virgin Islands Police Force, Officer Terrell Johnson, making his rounds around the dock. Lou whispered to Jake and Mike, "All right, boys, put on your best tourist face. This guy's with C.I.D. according to that patch on his arm. Let's give him nothing to write home about, okay?"

As the police officer walked past the bar, he glanced at the three sitting there engaged in conversation and turned away, seemingly not noticing anything out of the ordinary. What they didn't know was that as he rounded the corner of the building and moved out of sight and they gave a collective sigh of relief, he was already looking at two photographs he retrieved from his shirt pocket, got on his cell phone, and made a call to the other side of the dock where a photographer was engaged in taking pictures of tourists as they came to Customs for entry and registration.

Seeing who was calling, the photographer quickly answered his phone and moved himself into a position where he could see across the dock to Pusser's Bar. Nodding his head in acknowledgement, he put a new telescopic lens on his camera and zeroed in on the three men seated at the bar and began to shoot. He quickly downloaded the pictures to his laptop and e-mailed them as attachments to the officer still waiting around the corner. When they were received, the officer then e-mailed them on to his contact on St. John. The officer smiled as he continued his beat. If these men were who he thought they were, a substantial payday would be his, which meant quite more to him than doing his duty and assisting his police brethren in the U.S.V.I. in apprehending dangerous fugitives.

Mike noted all the shops around where they were sitting.

"You know what, Lou? It's time to get you a suit. You're about to become an attorney."

"You're kidding?" said Lou.

"Nope. As a matter of fact, you're going to be an attorney for Andre Bollinger's estate. I think it's high time you made an appointment with Adolphus Hamilton and explain to him that all those papers that are supposed to be filed tomorrow morning – that's not going to happen. Let's let Hamilton know his murder plan worked. He got what he wanted. Bollinger and his lawsuits are out of the way. I think he'd be more than happy to see you."

Walking around the dock they found a shop, and Mike bought Lou a linen suit, shirt, tie, and dress shoes, – everything he needed to look the respectable attorney. Given Lou's build, it was going to require some tailoring, but a little extra cash got a promise from the shop owner that he'd have it ready first thing in the morning. Stopping at a leather shop, they bought a portfolio to complete the ensemble.

"Looks like we need to find a place to stay the night," said Jake.

Out of habit, they looked at Lou.

"Yeah, yeah . . . I do know a guy. There's a place here called the Spy Glass. Let me make a call. I'll get us some rooms."

Lou came back to the two. "All right, my pal is going to take care of us. I also called another friend who flies for Seaborne Airlines. They fly out of the airport on Beef Island, just north of here, to the St. Croix airport. I've got us on a flight leaving tomorrow morning at 9:30 A.M. We'll arrive at St. Croix at 10:15."

"What about all the baggage we have locked away in the boat?"

"No problem. I already made arrangements. A friend will stow it away for us and get it to St. Croix."

Jake looked at Mike and shook his head.

"What can I say?" said Mike, "he's not your average bartender."

"All right," said Mike, "let's go back to Pusser's and finalize our plan. Then we have a call to make."

"To whom?" said Jake.

"Adolphus Hamilton. Our prominent attorney here needs to make an appointment for tomorrow morning."

Jake pulled Mike aside. "You know that toast we made about the underdog? You think we've got a shot to pull this off?"

"We don't have a choice, Jake," said Mike. "We have to find evidence that you didn't commit this murder, and the only way we can do that is find out who framed you . . . and when we find that out, we're going to find out who the true murderer is. Like I told you, we're just working a case . . . same as always."

"I don't know," said Jake. "It seems more than that with my ass on the line."

"Listen Jake, I've seen you go after people who have hurt other people, who are evil, with no regard for yourself, and you go after them with a vengeance and don't quit until you get them. This is no different. Don't forget . . . someone was murdered and somewhere and somehow this thing is tied to politics and money . . . just like always . . . and there's some bad guy out there calling the shots and we need to him bring down. You're a pawn on the chessboard in this one, but that doesn't mean we don't go after them the same way we always do. Now, quit feeling sorry for yourself and get a little bit of that righteous anger back and let's go get these bastards . . . all right?"

ST. CROIX

U.S. V.I.

CHAPTER 26

It was Sunday evening. The Adolphus Hamilton estate sat at the old site of an 18th century sugar mill located on a 500-ft. hilltop in the center of St. Croix. The guests had just finished dinner and strolled to the terrace for cigars and drinks. The phone could be heard ringing from inside, and a servant brought it out and gave it to Adolphus Hamilton.

"What? Well, do I have an opening? All right, put him in the slot and I'll see him in the morning. No more appointments, and I don't want bothered again this evening." With that, he hung up the phone. He would have to have a chat with his appointment secretary. The calls to him in his private time were becoming too frequent and he would have to set restrictions.

Just then, a phone rang on the terrace, as Mr. Dalton called his employer.

"What is it?!"

"I have information."

"Ah, Dalton. Finally. I hope you're reporting progress."

"As I suspected sir, the reports that Sullivan and Lang had fled the islands and were back in Miami were to mislead us. I just received photographic evidence that this afternoon they were in West End on Tortola with a third party whose identity I'm currently chasing down. I've tracked them to the Spy Glass Hotel and I'm sending in a team."

"Very good, Mr. Dalton, very good. I don't care about the others, but remember . . . I want Sullivan brought in alive. And Mr. Dalton . . ."

"Yes, sir?"

"I think it's time we clean up loose ends. Sullivan and Lang are not to be underestimated, nor is the influence they hold with the President and his staff. Make sure this is a police operation to recover an escaped fugitive and those who are killed simply lost their lives in a gun battle with the police. We have to remain isolated from this. After we have our meeting with Mr. Sullivan, he'll be sent to Golden Grove, where unfortunately, he'll be killed by an inmate who, naturally, will be killed by guards coming to Mr. Sullivan's rescue. Mr. Sullivan's escape only adds to the evidence of his guilt. Mr. Dalton, as long as we keep this under control and follow the plan, there will be no way any loose ends can be associated with us."

"I understand sir. It'll be taken care of."

"See that it is, Mr. Dalton. See that it is."

And with that, his employer ended the conversation and looked out over the island. And it was his island, and soon it would be the center of an independent nation, which he would control. The meeting he had in the afternoon with the PIVI had gone well. He had explained to them how the economic ties he was forging would give the new nation an economic clout in world markets that no one would ever see coming, and the recognition of the island's sovereignty would come from one Caribbean nation after another . . . and then the world.

With the money he would pour into their party, they would win the next election for territorial governor and immediately call for a referendum for independence. There had been some reluctance and outright hostility at his suggestion that Chief Prosecutor Donaldson be their candidate for governor. But as he clearly outlined how he would systematically destroy their party if they did not agree to his candidate, a majority came to see the light, and the vocal minority that was still disputing his decisions would gradually be eliminated.

He turned and looked to the other men sitting on the terrace. Representatives from Venezuela, Mexico, and the important islands in the Caribbean were all in attendance. They had come to learn if scientific breakthroughs made by Hamilton Labs were successful in real conditions, and all had agreed to the production and pricing guidelines he wanted to establish. He took a long drag on his cigar and then a sip of Cruzan Rum and smiled to himself. He was in command of the situation . . . exactly where he wanted to be.

"Good news?" asked one of the attendees.

"Indeed. We've located Sullivan and his friends, and my men are moving in to capture them."

"I still don't like it," said one of the other attendees. "This is way too public . . . and not necessary."

One of the other attendees started to rise, but he put a calming hand on his shoulder and he sat back down.

"Gentlemen, let me make something clear to you. Jake Sullivan has caused great suffering to the Hamilton family and the family's entitled to its revenge. Sullivan has put himself in the position of being a fugitive, only making him look more guilty. He will be arrested. He will be taken to Golden Grove, as was to occur, and there he will meet an untimely end. This will happen, and there is to be no argument. Do I make myself clear? Now gentlemen," he said, smiling, "this meeting is at an end, and I suggest everyone retire for the night."

There would be no more questions . . . no more challenges to his ultimate authority . . . and he smiled as he took another sip of rum.

TORTOLA

B.V.I.

CHAPTER 27

Mike, Jake and Lou had just arrived at their rooms in the Spy Glass when Lou abruptly left, indicating he had to go talk to his contact. Twenty minutes later he was back.

"Pack up boys. I think we've been made."

"What are you talking about?" said Mike.

"My friend from MI6 . . . after he dropped off his package, he took a walk to the other side of the dock. He noticed a photographer who was taking pictures of tourists coming into Customs, stop what he was doing, put a telescopic lens on his camera, and aim it right at us. He then downloaded the pictures he took to a computer. Our friend looked across the dock and that Royal Virgin Island Police Officer we saw . . . never moved once he turned the corner and we saw him disappear. He was standing there on his cell phone the whole time. Our guy thinks the photographer downloaded the pictures to him, and I can only guess where they went from there. Someone's coming after us. We can't do anything about it in this place. The hallway's a dead end, it's narrow, one entranceway. If they want us, they got us. So it's time to move."

"To where?" said Jake.

"My friend here, he dates a real estate agent. There's a villa up on the hill for sale that's empty. He's been able to get us a key. We can spend the night there and head for the airport in the morning.

But more importantly, he'll keep us apprised if anyone shows up here, and we'll know where we stand. Now let's go. We've got to move. If somebody's coming, they're probably on their way."

"Hey, we didn't even get a chance to unpack, so it's no problem," said Mike, lifting the duffle bag with all their equipment. "Let's go."

Lou's contact, who answered to the name Deke, took them up into the hills above the West End and entered a code at a gated entry and drove up a driveway to a villa, giving Lou the keys.

"Look, man, don't trash the place, and get out as soon as you can. Just leave the keys in the lock box."

"Don't worry. We'll be careful brother. We just need a place to lay our heads. We're out first thing in the morning. Thanks, man. I owe you."

"All right, we're even . . . understand? No more."

"I got you, brother. I got you. But do me one more. If they show up, let me know."

"Will do."

Quietly entering the villa, they moved into the living room, threw their gear on the floor, and each took a couch. Without even removing the dust covers, all three were asleep, the adrenaline on which they had been running easing, and exhaustion setting in.

CHAPTER 28

The three had been awake for several hours when they were surprised by the sound of a vehicle coming up the driveway. All had risen early, showered and shaved with toiletries they found in the guest bathrooms, and put on clean clothes, Lou looking every bit the attorney in his suit and tie. As promised, they cleaned up any mess they had made and stuffed the dirty towels in a garbage can they found outside. Jake and Mike had just got done saying to Lou he had obviously been mistaken, but they were thankful for the night's rest and the use of the house. They were going over the plan for the third time when the vehicle interrupted them.

The car braked hard and screeched to a stop and a young girl got out and ran to the door. She jumped back in fear as she opened it and saw three men, with guns pointed at her, in kneeling positions located at various angles to the doorway, ready to fire. She started to turn and run.

"Wait! Wait! It's okay! It's all right! Just cautious. Who are you?" said Mike.

"Look, I don't know who you guys are or what you're doing, but you've gotta get outta here! I can't be involved in this anymore," she said.

"What are you talking about?" said Mike. "What's wrong?"

"What's wrong?! Four armed men came to the Spy Glass last night looking for you three, and I'm scared to death they're gonna come looking for me too! That's what's wrong!"

"Son of a bitch!" said Lou. "I told Deke to call me if they showed up."

"You don't get it! Deke's dead!" she spat out. "He's dead! They beat him to death!"

Lou's eyes grew dark. His body stiffened and his left fist clenched. The gun dropped to his side, and he turned and walked away. Suddenly enraged, he turned and moved swiftly towards the girl.

"Do we know who they are? Anything? Is there anything to let us know who they are?"

"Just this," she said, and held up a photo she keyed in on her phone. "The guy that found Deke took a picture of this. It looks like Deke was trying to write something in his own blood."

The picture showed the base of a wall just above the molding and on it in red were two 'V's' – one pointing downward and one pointing upward.

"This is it? This is all we have?"

"Look, don't stand here and yell at me! Deke's dead because of you! They didn't show up here, did they? So he didn't tell them anything. He took his beating and he lost his life to protect your sorry ass! I'm leaving . . . and you get the hell outta here and don't come back!"

"Wait . . . wait," said Jake. "Let me see the picture." He looked at it and showed it to Mike and then stared at it some more, then closed the phone and gave it back to the girl. "Go ahead Miss . . . go on . . . go." And with that, she looked at them all with contempt, turned, slammed the door, got in her car, and squealing tire, she gunned it down the driveway.

"It was Vaughan," said Jake.

Lou turned on him. "How do you know that?"

"It's not two inverted Vs. The first one's a V. The second one is the beginning of an A. Vaughan . . . V – a – u – g – h – a – n. It's the first two letters of his name. That's what he was trying to tell us."

"But he didn't know Vaughan's name," said Lou.

"My guess," said Jake, "Vaughan told him. Vaughan wanted us to know he was there. He probably didn't realize how bad Deke was hurt and that he'd get word to us when someone found him." Jake shook his head. "The poor bastard did, just not the way Vaughan thought it would happen."

Lou paced back and forth for several minutes, the anger rising. He knew the girl was right. He knew Deke was dead because of him, and now he was going to make them pay.

"Let's get our gear and get the hell out of here! We've got a plane to catch, and we've got business to take care of!"

Mike moved in front of him. "Hold on. Look, you asked to be a part of this, and I tried to talk you out of it. Remember what you told me about Paula? When we take on these jobs, we sometimes lose good people, but we still have to take on the jobs. I came here to get Jake out of this jackpot. That was my primary goal and it still is. It looks like the only way we're going to do that is to take these bastards down, but I still have to get evidence that he's innocent. We'll get these guys, I promise you. But we have to do it the way I say. Are you going to be able to walk into that room this morning and do what you have to do?"

"Yeah, I got it. Sorry. Don't worry, I'll do what I gotta do, Jake. We'll get you outta this."

Jake nodded his head. Mike looked at Jake and then back at Lou.

"All right, let's get going."

"One thing, though," said Lou. "After we know Jake's clear, with you or without you . . . I'm taking these guys down. And don't even think of trying to stop me." And with that he picked up his bag and headed out the door.

They walked a short distance down the hill until they came to the dock and were able to hail a cab to take them across Ridge Road the length of the island to East End, across the causeway over Beef Island Channel, and arrived at the airport on Beef Island.

Once they got out of the cab, Mike and Jake headed for the Seaborne Terminal. Lou, as planned, headed for the charter area. There was a charter leaving this morning and he had made arrangements with the pilot, with whom he indicated he had "done some work" in the past, who was willing to carry their equipment and other gear on his plane to St. Croix. He agreed he would leave it in a locker at the airport and the key for the locker would be kept under the name of Lou Becker, awaiting pickup, and they would retrieve their equipment when they arrived. It wasn't long before Lou joined the other two at the Seaborne Terminal and at approximately 9:30 A.M., they took off for St. Croix.

Once in the air, Lou sat in stony silence looking out the window, and Jake made one attempt to break through. "Hey, Lou, I just thought of something. What's going to happen with your boat?"

Without even turning from the porthole, Lou replied, "Don't worry about it. It's being taken care of."

With that, Jake looked at Mike and shook his head, and for the rest of the flight, all three were quiet.

ST. CROIX

CHAPTER 29

Arriving at the airport in St. Croix, they immediately went to pick up the key, with Lou fitting the description of Lou Becker that had been given to the attendant, and took their gear out of the locker. Using their forged documents, they rented a car. Once they were seated, Mike behind the wheel, and before they had pulled out of the rental space, Lou surprised them by speaking.

"Look guys . . . I don't want you to worry. I've got this. I know the plan cold, and I know what we have to do."

"You know Dalton may well be in that room with you?" said Mike.

"I know. I'll be cool. I can wait."

"Good enough," said Mike. "Let's do this," and he started the car and headed out on the Melvin H. Evans Highway, retracing the route he took to Christianstad when he met with the Burkes.

They found a parking space on Company Street. Lou put on the glasses and made sure the camera in the flag pin he put on his lapel was working. Jake took the ring and walked a hundred yards down from the car and spoke, and the pick-up was clear. Getting back in the car, he gave the ring to Lou, and they checked the laptop to make sure it was picking up sight and sound. Lou then inserted the minute earpiece that fit deep into his ear and couldn't be observed by casual observation, so he would be able to receive directions from Jake and/or Mike, seated in the car on the street below.

As Lou was ready to leave, Mike stopped him.

"Lou, look, I know you want these guys, and like I told you, we'll get them. But we've gotta make them come out in the open. Just tell them what we've talked about and we'll see how they react. We've gotta figure they'll know who you are from the photograph our friendly police officer had taken . . . or at least they'll know you're with us. They'll have to wonder what you are doing coming into their ballpark, especially once you let them know we know who they are. So just stick to the plan, all right?"

"Yeah, Mike. I got it. This isn't my first rodeo."

"I know. I know. But it's personal now. That sometimes makes a difference."

"Hell Mike. One way or another, it's always personal. You know that. I gotta go." And with that, he was out of the car and heading for the offices of Hamilton Industries.

CHAPTER 30

The blonde receptionist looked up from her desk to see a tall, handsome man with curly black hair walking toward her. Putting on her best smile, she asked, "Can I help you, sir?"

"Yes, please. My name is Sinclair Bassett of the law firm of Singleton, Bassett and Thomas in Miami. I called last evening to make an appointment to see Mr. Hamilton."

"Does he know what this is about?" asked the receptionist, still smiling.

Smiling back, the attorney said, "I represent the Estate of Andre Bollinger. Mr. Bollinger had entered into some litigation involving Mr. Hamilton, and given Mr. Bollinger's death, that litigation is to be terminated. I wanted to explain how this would work to Mr. Hamilton and advise him that no further action on his part would be necessary."

"Please have a seat, Mr. Bassett, and I'll let Mr. Hamilton know that you're here."

"Thank you very much," said Mr. Bassett as he took a seat in the waiting area.

Fifteen minutes later the young lady, exiting her desk slowly and making sure she presented a profile so that Mr. Bassett could appreciate all aspects of her person, walked over and stopped, much closer than necessary to Mr. Bassett.

"Please follow me, Mr. Bassett, and I'll take you in to Mr. Hamilton."

Mr. Bassett couldn't help but smile to himself as he walked down the hallway, watching the receptionist's hips move to and fro, sure that the emphasis was added for him, until they reached the large, mahogany carved door. The receptionist moved to the side and opened the door and gestured Mr. Bassett in, leaving little space for him to enter the office without brushing up against her.

"Thank you very much."

"Anytime," said the young receptionist, and closed the door behind her.

Bassett turned and saw an older man with a perfectly styled mane of white hair, immaculately dressed, rise from behind his desk.

"Mr. Hamilton?" asked Bassett.

"Yes. And you must be Mr. Bassett?"

"Indeed I am, sir," he said, moving forward and extending his hand.

Hamilton's grip, even for his age, was still firm. As the handshake ended, Hamilton gestured for Bassett to sit down, and he resumed his seat behind the desk.

Opening the leather portfolio he brought with him and taking a pen out of his inside coat pocket, Bassett looked down at what was really an empty sheet of paper and began to speak.

"Mr. Hamilton, my name is Sinclair Bassett. I'm with the law firm of Singleton, Bassett and Thomas in Miami. We have been hired to represent the Estate of Andre Bollinger."

"Ah, yes. Mr. Bollinger. A tragedy," said Hamilton. "His murder has been a great distress to the people of these islands."

"I'm sure it has, Mr. Hamilton. I've only gotten some of the horrid details of the crime. Am I correct that the murderer has escaped and is on the loose?"

"Temporarily. But it's only a matter of time. He'll be caught and justice will prevail."

"I certainly hope so. Sir, I am not sure what your relationship was with Mr. Bollinger, but I know he had initiated certain legal actions against you relative to your purchase of the closed refinery on the southern side of the island, and I believe a petition for removal to federal court had also been filed."

"Yes, yes. Well, with Mr. Bollinger's death, those items were stayed by an order of the Superior Court. As a matter of fact, a hearing was supposed to be held this morning, but obviously, given the circumstances, we aren't sure what's going to happen."

"Well, that is why I'm here, sir. I wanted to let you know that after a review of all the documentation, and after discussions with the heirs of Mr. Bollinger's estate, we have determined that the action will be settled and discontinued, with prejudice, and all legal actions involving Hamilton Industries and yourself will be terminated."

"Well, I'm certainly glad to hear that," said Hamilton, sitting back in his chair and tenting his hands in front of him. "You know, Mr. Bollinger and I weren't enemies. As a matter of fact, I had great respect for the man. We just had somewhat of a different opinion as to how to best revitalize the islands and give the most benefit to their inhabitants, and I'm sorry it took his death to bring these matters to a conclusion."

Just then, a panel in the far wall opened and Vaughan walked in. For just a brief moment, Lou felt the anger rise. He wanted to leap out of the chair and grab Vaughan by the throat, but he calmed himself, knowing what he had to do. It was time to play the game, time to see the reactions of the enemy, and see what the next move would be.

"Ah, Mr. Dalton . . . I'm glad you could join us. Mr. Bassett, this is Thomas Dalton, my head of security. This is Sinclair Bassett, an attorney from Miami who has just informed me that all of the legal proceedings filed by Mr. Bollinger prior to his death are going to be terminated and discontinued by the heirs of the estate . . . correct, Mr. Bassett?"

"That is correct, sir," said Bassett, locking eyes with Vaughan, and seeing in those eyes evidence that Vaughan recognized who he was.

Vaughan walked over and extended his hand. "Nice to meet you, Mr. Bassett, is it?"

"Yes, exactly," said Bassett, standing up and grasping Vaughan's hand, exerting as much strength and pressure as he could. The two men stood like that for some time, each staring into the other's eyes. Finally, Vaughan let go and moved back to stand beside Hamilton, behind the desk.

Bassett looked out the window. "Beautiful offices, Mr. Hamilton. Quite a view."

"Yes, I have worked hard for what I have attained, but I've been most fortunate, also."

"May I?" said Bassett, extending his hand around the room. "Please do," said Hamilton.

Keeping the pen in the palm of his hand, where he hoped it wouldn't be noticed, Bassett walked along the various walls of the office, peering intently at certain artifacts, clicking the pen as he went, until he came to the portrait of a beautiful young woman in an elegant frame, alone on the far wall.

"What a beautiful portrait," said Bassett. "A family member, I presume?" he said, looking at Hamilton. He could see Hamilton tense . . . his whole demeanor change, and then he regained his composure.

"Yes, it's a portrait of my daughter . . . a beautiful girl."

"Beautiful indeed," said Bassett, moving on. Once he completed his tour of the office, he resumed his seat. He reached in the portfolio and jotted something down, making it look as if the pen had been in the portfolio the entire time, then put the pen back in his inside coat pocket. "Well, Mr. Hamilton, I believe that concludes our business. I will file the necessary papers immediately, make sure you are provided with copies, take care of the court docket, and the matter will be at an end."

"Very good, Mr. Bassett. I appreciate you taking this action. As I said, I am glad this matter is being concluded without the need for further litigation, and I want you to give my sympathies to Mr. Bollinger's family members and tell them of my deep sorrow at what has occurred."

Standing up and extending his hand to Hamilton, Bassett said, "I will do that, sir. The family was somewhat unsure as to how you would react to these things. For some reason, they had the feeling that you had a deep-seeded animosity toward Mr. Bollinger . . . that he was somehow standing in the way of your economic plans for the future of the island and that there was some type of political dispute, also. I'm sure they'll be glad to hear that was not the case and that this was merely a business dispute that sometimes occurs."

The words caught Hamilton off guard, if only for a moment. He looked at Vaughan.

"At any rate, I will be on my way," said Bassett, turning and moving toward the door. It was when he had his hand on the knob, ready to open the door, that he turned once again and looked at Hamilton and Vaughan. "Oh, and I truly hope that whoever was involved with Mr. Bollinger's murder is brought to justice, as we discussed. Again, it was a pleasure, Mr. Hamilton. It was very nice meeting you, Mr. Vaughan."

Hamilton started out of his chair at the comment. Vaughan placed a hand on his shoulder and held him in place and smiled back at Bassett. "I'm sorry, Mr. Bassett, you must have heard incorrectly. My name is Dalton, Thomas Dalton."

"That's right," said Bassett. "Excuse me. I don't know what I was thinking . . . probably involved in something else I have to take care of today. Getting ahead of myself, it seems. Well, once again, thank you." And with that, Bassett exited the office and made his way past the receptionist. "Good day, and thank you," he said.

"Anytime," said the receptionist, with the same smile.

Bassett was no sooner out the front door that he pulled at the tie around his neck, opened his collar and took off his jacket, and headed for the car parked down the street. The transformation only took a moment, and just like that, Sinclair Bassett was no more . . . and Lou Caravaggio was walking down the street.

CHAPTER 31

As soon as Bassett was gone, Hamilton leaned back at his desk and spoke to Dalton.

"So what do you think of the barrister? At least that's an issue we won't have to deal with."

"Don't be so sure," said Vaughan, leaning over to work the computer on Hamilton's desk. "He's no barrister."

Hamilton sat upright in his chair. "What do you mean?"

"Look. The photograph I got from our friend from his contact on Tortola . . . look at the man on the left."

Hamilton put on his reading glasses and stared at the screen and then looked up at Vaughan. "It's him." Hamilton sat back with a puzzled look on his face. "What the hell kind of game are they playing?"

"They want to let us know what they know. That's why he called me Vaughan. They know who I am. All that talk about justice being served . . . they know we're involved. The question is how much do they know and what evidence do they have?"

"You have any other brilliant plans? Something that won't end like that debacle at the hotel last night?"

"We all agree . . . Sullivan and Lang know what they're doing and are not to be underestimated, and I guarantee you, the barrister is definitely ex-military. They knew they'd been spotted, and they knew I'd find them. They set me up, made me waste my time and resources while they were getting a good night's rest somewhere else. One thing's for certain . . . they're all here."

"How can you be so sure? I must admit, I don't have a great deal of faith left in your strategies."

"Then it's a good thing my strategies are not your call. Look, I know what I'm doing. They can't hide anymore, so they're going on the offensive. Now they want to see what we'll do."

"What you better do," said Hamilton, "is hunt them down and find them . . . and get me Sullivan!"

"I'll get you Sullivan, and I'll take care of the others myself. This is going to end . . . and it's going to end now."

Vaughan turned and started to go back to the panel from where he had entered when Hamilton stopped him.

"By the way, I understand, Mr. Vaughan, that the hotel on Tortola wasn't your only failure last night."

"I sent men to the house last night. They weren't home. I have men combing through their personal history now. We'll find them, and it will be taken care of."

Hamilton was reading some documents and never lifted his head. "I certainly hope so, Mr. Vaughan. Our friends have a certain way of dealing with liabilities. Ensure that you don't become one."

Vaughan felt the anger rising. "Same as always . . . old men sit at desks and give orders while we bloody ourselves. The life I have chosen," he thought as he left to prepare for the work at hand.

CHAPTER 32

By agreement, once Lou left the vehicle, Jake and Mike moved it to a side street, well-hidden among a line of parked cars, trucks, and vans. It took Lou almost a half an hour to get back to the car. He knew that Vaughan would send someone after him, knowing that he would lead them to Mike and Jake, so he took various routes, doubled back, and used the skills he had learned to evade a tail.

When he finally arrived back at the car and climbed into the back seat, Jake never raised his head, staring intently at the photographs Lou had sent back to the laptop.

"We'd better move," said Lou. "I don't think that tail they had on me is going to stay lost forever. Where's Mike?"

Jake was staring intently at the laptop and it was as if he didn't hear.

"Jake! Where's Mike?"

"Oh, sorry. He went out to see if he could find an address for the Burkes."

"What's got you so interested? What did you see?"

"It's this photograph on the wall."

"Oh, that beautiful young girl?"

"Yeah, there's something about her . . . something familiar."

"Are you sure?"

"No, I can't be sure, but it's in my gut. There's something . . ."

"You think that's the tie-in?"

"I don't know. I just . . . I never met her, she's not Alaina, and that was my only contact with the islands. I don't know what it is. There's just something about her."

"She's damn beautiful, that's for sure."

"I watched in there," said Jake. "You did a hell of a job. I think you've got 'em rattled."

"Let's hope. And let's hope rattling the cage gets us somewhere."

Just then, Mike came back, opened the door and slid behind the wheel. "Found it! A young couple, wearing Hamilton badges on their lab coats . . . they work with Mrs. Burke. I was a friend of the family down here on vacation and wanted to surprise them. Found out two things. One, she's not at work today, and two, they gave me directions to their house."

"Let's go!" said Lou, as Mike started the car and pulled out. "Jake, tell Mike about what you saw."

"What is it Jake?" asked Mike.

"There's a portrait on the wall in the office of a young girl. There's just something about her, it's like I know her. It's not Alaina. I've never seen her, but there's something about her that I recognize. I don't know what it is."

"Keep thinking. It'll come to you, Jake. It always does."

Mike followed the directions he had been given and took Route 75 out of Christianstad, then turned onto 62, and then turned onto Lawry Hill Road, past Lang's Observatory, and came to Lawry Hill. The view as they wound their way up was magnificent over Buck Island Channel, toward Buck Island and beyond. And Jake, for a brief moment, took in the beauty of the islands in spite of what had happened and what was to come. His thoughts were broken by Mike announcing, "There it is," as he pulled onto a dirt road and headed up to a white island-style house, pulled into the driveway in front of the house, and parked.

As the three got out, looking around them, Mike moved to the front door and knocked. No answer. He knocked again. Still no answer. Just then, a voice down the road called out.

"Can I help you fellas?"

Putting his hand behind his back on the Glock and noticing that Lou was doing the same, Mike turned in the direction of the voice and saw a middle-aged lady with a walking stick and a broad-brimmed straw hat strolling up a path that opened through the woods on the side of the house. She was holding what looked like a manila envelope and staring down at something as she walked.

"We're looking for Mr. and Mrs. Burke, ma'am. Do you know where they might be?" asked Jake.

"They're not here."

"Yeah, we gathered that, ma'am, but do you have any idea where they are?"

The woman kept coming closer, until she was standing right in front of Jake, and he could see that she was looking down at a newspaper, then looking back at him. "You're a little bit scruffy around the edges, but you're him. You're Jake Sullivan, aren't you?"

Jake looked at Mike and Lou.

Mike said, "Ma'am, who are you, if I may ask?"

"I'm a friend of Andrea's . . . neighbor down the path. She gave me this photograph."

Jake looked at it. It was a photo of him that had appeared in a great many newspapers after he and Mike had discovered Meyer Lanski's missing millions.

"They told me that you'd probably be coming, and if I found you, I was supposed to give you this envelope."

Jake opened the envelope and read. When he was done, he looked at Lou and Mike. "Listen to this:

'Mr. Sullivan, first I sincerely apologize for taking part in the scheme to have you arrested and convicted for the murder of Andre Bollinger. I did so because of a mixture of greed, love for my family, and duress from Adolphus Hamilton and his henchman,Thomas Dalton. My wife and I have a daughter, Angela. She's only four and she suffers from Cystic Fibrosis. My brother lives in St. Louis, and he told me that the St. Louis Children's Hospital had developed new methods of treating Cystic Fibrosis and preparing children as young as Angela for lung transplants. Some-how, that information got in the hands of Adolphus Hamilton. He called me into his office one day and told me that he had a couple things that he needed done, and if I cooperated, he would pay for all the expenses of sending Angela to St. Louis, doing the necessary work-up, and preparing her for lung transplants. He also made it very clear that if I refused, not only would we lose our jobs, but that there would be far more severe penalties. That's why I gave my statement about seeing you on the beach that night. I now know that I was a fool. With the information we have about your lack of involvement in the murder, I now know that Hamilton will not let us live. Dalton's been following us, and it's only a matter of time. Hopefully, when you get this information, we'll still be alive. We are staying with my wife's sister on Virgin Gorda at her home in Soldier Bay. Here are the directions. I know this is a lot to ask, given what we've done, but please come and help us. I can provide you with evidence of Hamilton's illegal involvement in politics, and my wife and I can give you information on what the lab has produced and what he intends to do, that could well create a worldwide economic panic. I'm sorry, but there's no one else I trust.'

And it's signed Marcus Burke."

Mike looked at Lou. "What are we waiting for? Let's go."

"I'm sorry, ma'am. I never got your name."

"Mims. Addie Mims. Mr. Sullivan, I know about you. I think you're a good man. These are nice folks, and that Hamilton is a no good son of a bitch! I'm sure he's behind those boys who came sniffing around here last night."

"What's that?" asked Mike.

"Yeah, four or five of them pulled in here last night looking for Andrea and her husband. I come up the path real quiet like and they never saw me. I saw 'em in the headlights of the car. Tall, sandy-haired fella . . . mean lookin'. Three or four other guys. Walked all over the place. Hell, they broke in the back door. Saw 'em running around inside with flashlights. Then they came out and took off. Looked like the same group of men that took the daughter, Angela, away four or five days ago."

Mike said, "Miss Mims, did Mr. and Mrs. Burke have a habit of telling people about her sister's place?"

"I don't think so. I just found out about it from the letter. I didn't even know she had a sister, and hell, we've been close for years."

Jake looked at Mike and Lou. "We have a chance they don't know about this. If we get there first and we get this evidence . . ."

Mike finished the sentence. "I can call Bates and get the troops sent in."

Jake turned to Miss Mims. "Thank you much, ma'am. I appreciate it. I'll do everything I can. I promise."

"Good enough for me. Good luck boys." And with that, she turned and headed back down the path.

Walking back to the car, Lou said, "I wouldn't mind bringing that old bird along. Give me a second fellas, I've got to make a phone call." And with that, he moved off to the side of the path.

Coming back, Jake spoke up. "What's the plan?"

"Head back to the airport," said Lou. "Go back out on the road, go the way we were going. Just keep following the signs for 62. That'll take us right up to Melvin Evans Highway and back to the airport. Air Sunshine flies out of there to Virgin Gorda. It's the quickest way there. If the schedule is still the same, there's a flight we can catch at 3:30 that will get us there at approximately 6:00 o'clock. We'll have to charter it. I know one of the pilots – he'll help us out."

Jake turned around. "How the hell do you know all this?" asked Jake. Answering his own question . . . "Never mind. I know, 'you know a guy and you did a job.'"

Lou just sat back and smiled. Jake looked at Mike and shook his head.

Mike said, "Just like I said . . . not just your average bartender."

Then they headed for the airport.

VIRGIN GORDA

B.V.I.

CHAPTER 33

While waiting at the airport for their chartered flight to Virgin Gorda, Mike had made a decision. He made his argument to Jake and Lou and grudgingly, they agreed.

Hitting a number into his burner phone, Mike waited as the phone on the other end began to ring.

"Bill Adams," came the voice on the other end of the line.

"Bill, this is Mike."

There was a pause.

"Well, well . . . if it isn't my favorite fugitive. I sure as hell hope you called me to tell me where you are so I can come and get you and end all this."

"Bill, I'm asking you for a favor. Give me a couple minutes to tell you what's going on."

Again, a pause.

"You have two minutes, Mike, and then I'm coming after you."

"Fair enough," said Mike, and he proceeded to tell him what they had learned, where they were, and where they were headed.

"Sounds like a pretty big conspiracy theory," said Adams.

"Look, Bill, there's two separate things going on here. There's no question somebody used Jake. And there's a reason he was picked for this, and we haven't figured that one out yet, but Bollinger's death is part of a much wider scheme. And I'm telling you, it's about politics, oil, and money . . . and at the center of it is Adolphus Hamilton."

"So believing he was the big bear in the woods, you decided to go poke him with a stick to see if he'd start chasing you?"

"Something like that," said Mike. "Look Bill, the Burkes are running scared. This guy says he has evidence that'll clear Jake and let us get to Hamilton and stop whatever's going on. But no matter what it is, if it comes from me, Kirkland and Bates are gonna require more proof of its authenticity and accuracy, and that's gonna take time, and that's time we don't have. Hamilton's right-hand man, a guy that goes by the name of Dalton, his name is really Aiden Vaughan. He's a mercenary. I've seen his type before – stone-cold killer. Call your contacts at Interpol. Check him out. I have no doubt he's comin' after us . . . maybe after the Burkes, too . . . and we have to get to them first."

"All right, Mike, I gave you your two minutes. Let's say you're right about everything you told me. What do you want from me?"

"Meet us at the sister's house on Virgin Gorda. If there is evidence, I want to turn it over to you, and if there needs to be some type of official action to protect these folks and the evidence they have, I want you to be the one calling the shots. I want you to meet us on Virgin Gorda, find out what the Burkes have, and help us finish this. I'll give you directions."

"And what if I don't buy their story?"

"Then I guess you'll be a hero for arresting two infamous fugitives."

Another pause.

"Shit Mike! You've been a pain in the ass as long as I've known you!"

"And?" asked Mike.

"What do you think? Give me the directions so I can be on my way."

CHAPTER 34

The three men tried to get some rest during the two-hour flight from St. Croix to Virgin Gorda, but rest was hard to come by, especially for Mike and Jake, who both wondered what evidence the Burkes would have and whether it would be good enough.

Lou got out of his seat and walked to the cockpit and spoke to the pilot.

"We're about fifteen minutes out. My buddy called ahead. There'll be a ride waiting for us with the sister's address already in the GPS."

Mike and Jake looked at each other and just shook their heads.

"That's it boys. Not so down," said Lou. "This is the break we've been waiting for."

"I hope you're right," said Jake.

"C'mon," said Lou. "You know how it works. You can feel it when that big break is comin.'"

Jake turned and looked out the porthole. They were descending now, soon to land, and Lou was right . . . he could always feel it when a big break was coming. That was the problem . . . this time he just wasn't sure.

CHAPTER 35

After landing at the airport right next to the water of Taylor's Bay, they found a Range Rover that had been left for them and turned on the GPS. Following North Sound Road, they made their way up the spine of Virgin Gorda, past Black Point, and following the coast, they arrived at the cut off for Soldier Bay.

The house was a typical Caribbean design, set on a slope overlooking the bay.

Lou, who was driving, pulled the Range Rover into a circular drive and parked, and all three exited the vehicle. Just then the front door of the home opened and Marcus Burke appeared on the porch, holding a rifle.

"Well, Mr. Sullivan, I see you've met my neighbor. C'mon inside. We have a lot to talk about."

CHAPTER 36

The interior of the home was neat and clean. Andrea Burke sat on a sofa and her husband went over and sat beside her, motioning to three chairs, and Lou, Mike and Jake sat. Marcus Burke looked directly at Jake.

"Mr. Sullivan, I owe you an apology. I'm sorry for the part I played in what has happened to you, but you have to understand, I didn't have much of a choice . . . and neither did my wife."

"Why the change of heart?" asked Jake.

"I wish I could say it was a guilty conscience, but really it's a matter of self-preservation."

"What do you mean?" asked Mike.

"Let me start at the beginning. As you know, I work as an accountant for Hamilton Industries. For whatever reason, old man Hamilton took a liking to me and started to put a great deal of trust in me. I became the accountant that handled the books that no one else saw – the political payoffs, the deals with foreign investors, and the payoff to local politicians and police."

"But why were you and your wife picked to be the witnesses? To say you saw me coming up the hill from the murder scene?" asked Jake.

"It was our little girl," said Mrs. Burke. "Angela is four years old. She has Cystic Fibrosis. Mr. Hamilton agreed to transport her to the home of Marcus's brother in St. Louis. The St. Louis Children's Hospital has one of the best programs in the world for potential lung transplants and other treatments for the disease. He agreed to pay all costs for transporting her there and for all the medical care she would need. You have to understand," said Mrs. Burke, beginning to sob, "our last visit to her doctor didn't go well. She doesn't have long if she doesn't get help. We couldn't sit back and watch our baby die."

Lou spoke. "So Hamilton told you that if you would do what he wanted he'd take care of your daughter?"

"That," said Marcus, "and the implied threat that if we didn't, things would go very badly for us."

"So," said Mike, "you're telling me that you are the bookkeeper for Hamilton's illegal enterprises. That still doesn't tie him to Bollinger's murder, or in any way tell us why he's after Jake."

"There's more to this story, Mr. Lang. My wife is a chemist in the lab. For the past several years they've been working on a process that will allow the use of a liquid palomar to take the place of natural gas as a reinjection medium in the drilling for crude oil."

"I'm already lost," said Mike.

Mrs. Burke spoke up. "Think of it this way, Mr. Lang . . . Venezuela has been working on natural gas production since 1999. In 2005 it held an off-shore natural gas bidding round to award off-shore drilling rights off Falcon State in the western part of the country. Initial drillings were not very successful, but recently one of the largest fields of recoverable natural gas has been discovered at this site. The company that won the bidding rights in 2005 was a subsidiary of Hamilton Industries. The problem is that most of Venezuela's natural gas is used as a reinjection agent to allow them to pump more crude oil. When you find an underground reservoir of oil and you tap it and begin to drill, the pressure decreases, so you need to fill that cavity with something so the pressure increases and the drilling becomes more efficient and you produce more oil. That agent has always been natural gas. The process is called reinjection. What we at the lab discovered was a liquid palomar that can be used in place of natural gas for the reinjection process at half the cost than the use of natural gas entails."

"And what's that have to do," said Jake, "with what we're involved in?"

Marcus Burke once again spoke up. "It's important because of what I discovered in the course of my duties. Hamilton Industries has entered into a contract with the state-run production companies in Venezuela. He's begun selling the palomar he produces at a rate that will allow them, based upon the lower cost they will have for reinjection, to sell their oil at an amount drastically below the world selling price and also sell natural gas in liquid form, since they no longer have to use it for reinjection."

"But, why?" said Jake. "He could sell the palomar for more money and make a greater profit. Why take a loss?"

"Because," said Burke, "the key to the whole thing is that all of the crude oil and liquefied natural gas produced by Venezuela is contracted to be refined at the oil refinery he plans to reopen on St. Croix."

"And the guy standing in the way of the refinery opening was Bollinger," said Mike. "He was the one standing in the way of Hamilton making a fortune."

"It's more than that," said Burke. "I have records of payouts to critical members of the PIVI. Hamilton was taking over the party. He was going to merge it with the party he supported all these years and run Donaldson again for Territorial Governor. With the support of the Republican Party, Donaldson's a shoe-in. Unknown to Hamilton, I've listened in on some of his meetings and taken notes. As soon as Donaldson gets elected Territorial Governor, he's going to go forward with a referendum for independence. Given

Hamilton's money, backing from the PIVI, and the Republican Party – which is already in his pocket – it will win by a landslide."

Lou spoke up. "Sounds like Hamilton will be in a position to make even more money."

"You're missing the point," said Burke. "It's not just the money. If Hamilton pulls this off, he'll be the duly elected President of a new independent country, and if he's successful in what he plans to do with Venezuela, that country will be the primary distributor of processed oil and liquid natural gas to the entire world."

Looking at Jake, Burke went on, "Given the instability in the Middle East, the destruction of the price structure that will ensue as to the world oil market might be just enough to light the powder keg."

Jake spoke up. "Okay, Mr. Burke. Let's say we buy what you're selling. It's still going to be your word against Hamilton's."

Burke looked down at the ground and then looked up and smiled. "Not exactly, Mr. Sullivan. I kept two ledgers, one Hamilton's and one mine, and notes of all the meetings."

"Christ," said Jake, "that's the evidence we need! Where is it?"

Mr. Burke got up and moved to an ornately carved wooden desk that sat in the corner of the room. He knelt down at the side of the desk and put his thumb in a notch, lifting the carved side up and out, revealing a false wall between it and the runners for the drawer. From that space he removed a narrow, black binded book and a file folder and brought them over to where Jake was sitting.

"Here, Mr. Sullivan. I believe this is what you need to prove your innocence."

CHAPTER 37

Just then, a voice came loud and clear from off the front porch. Mr. Burke froze, as Jake, Mike, and Lou moved to the front windows.

"Mr. Sullivan and Mr. Lang," the voice repeated, "you need to come with us. We have a warrant for your arrest."

They looked outside to see four men in uniforms of the U.S. Virgin Islands Police Department, and in the center of them stood Aiden Vaughan. There was no vehicle.

"They must have parked at the bottom of the hill and made their way up so we wouldn't hear them," said Burke.

"Nice uniforms," said Mike. "Looks like you were right, Mr. Burke. The local police seem to be working for Hamilton Industries."

"Yeah, and I don't think arrest is really what they're interested in," said Jake. "More like execution."

Vaughan spoke again. "You have two minutes to come outside with the ledger and the other documents . . . or I'm afraid we'll have to come inside . . . and we'll come in firing! I know Mr. and Mrs. Burke are in there . . . obviously being held hostage by you . . . oh yes, and your friend, the would-be attorney. He also needs to come with us. I would hate to see anything happen to Mr. and Mrs. Burke based upon you making the wrong decision. Two minutes!"

Jake said, "How the hell did they know about the ledger?"

Lou spoke up. "They've been listening somehow. This was all a setup. I wondered why my pursuit when I left the office was less than I thought it would be. They wanted us to come here. They wanted us to lead them to the Burkes. They wanted to find out what information they had and what they were going to do."

"And that's how they know about the ledger," said Mike. "Vaughan played us."

Marcus Burke was now looking out the window, standing next to Mike. "What'd you call him?"

"His name's Aiden Vaughan."

"I always thought his name was Dalton."

"That's the name he's using. He's a mercenary hired by Hamilton to do his dirty work."

Burke shook his head. "Yeah, that's Hamilton all right. Always in the background. Always out of the picture."

It was one of those moments Jake had when he was trying to analyze evidence, when there was something there but he couldn't quite put his finger on it, and then it would hit him, just as it did now.

"Mike, get Eva on your phone."

"What? Now?"

"Just do it! Get Eva on your phone."

"Eva, it's Mike. Hold on. Jake wants to talk to you."

"Jake, I was so worried! Are you okay?"

"I'm fine Eva, but not now. Just listen to me. The picture you took of Mike sitting at my desk when I first left to come down here . . . did you save it on your phone?"

"I think so."

"Look . . . look and see. Find it."

Eva came back on the line. "Yeah, it's right here, sweetie, why?"

"Look carefully at the photograph. Is the credenza behind Mike visible?"

"It is."

"Is the award I got from Tampa on the second shelf?"

"You mean that crazy looking knife thing?"

"Yeah, exactly."

"Yeah, it's sitting right there."

"Send that photograph to Jason Bates with this message: "Murder weapon of Andre Bollinger still in my office while I'm on my way to the Virgin Islands. See time stamp.""

"Jake that's wonderful! It proves you didn't do it!"

"Let's hope so Eva. Get that to him right away, would you please?"

"I will. You and Mike okay?"

"For the moment, but I can't talk. I'll talk to you later."

And with that, he shut off the phone. Jake looked to see Mike staring at him and just shrugged his shoulders.

"This whole time," said Mike, "we had evidence that you didn't do this?"

"What can I say?" said Jake, "it just came to me."

"It's bad enough even here in paradise you have me involved in another world crisis . . . at least you could speed up your powers of deduction," said Mike.

Jake swept his arm around the room. "I've been busy with other things. Let's worry about the guys outside right now."

"All right guys! Enough! Let's get the Burkes to the back of the house and get ready to fight these guys. If we give up, they're going to die. We're all armed. At least we have a chance . . ."

At that point, Lou was interrupted by Vaughan calling from outside.

"Thirty seconds gentlemen! And just in case you thought I was bluffing, take a look out the window!"

One of the men had put what looked like a bazooka on his shoulder and it was pointed at the house.

"Christ!" said Lou. "They have an RPG! It'll make this place a fireball and destroy everyone and everything in it."

"So much for a gun fight," said Mike.

Just then, Mike put up his hand for quiet, moved over, and tapped Burke on the shoulder and motioned for him to follow him. They moved to the rear of the house to the bathroom. Mike entered, pulled Burke close, cupping his ear, and whispered, "Is there another way out of here?"

Burke responded in the same fashion to Mike. "There's an escape hatch under the rug in the kitchen floor. It leads to the crawl space beneath the house, and there's a piece of lattice work on a hinge. It opens to the back, towards the jungle."

"All right, you and your wife are going to get out of here. Get into the jungle and hide. There's a guy named Bill Adams. He's with the FBI. He'll be here, and he'll find you. Go with him. He'll make sure you're safe. Now get moving."

Burke tapped Mike on the shoulder and motioned him to follow him. Quietly, he went to a side wall in the hall and got down on his knee, and as quietly as he could, began to unscrew the grate that covered one of the vents for the air conditioning. Taking off the cover and reaching inside, he pulled out what appeared to be an identical ledger and file folder to the one he had given Jake. Getting up, he whispered to Mike, "Just in case . . . I made two."

Mike smiled and patted him on the shoulder. "We owe you, Mr. Burke."

With that, Mike took off the wristband he was wearing and gave it to Burke and whispered again, "GPS tracker. This will find us. Give it to Adams. Now get your wife and get out of here."

Quietly they went back to the living room. Mike motioned for everyone to be quiet and pointed to the second ledger and held up his hand with the number two, and then motioning for everyone to follow him, and at the same time yelling as loud as he could, "Give us a minute Vaughan! We're coming out! But I want your word you won't hurt the Burkes!"

"As long as you bring that ledger and Sullivan and the attorney are with you, you have my word!"

Motioning for everyone to follow, Burke led the way into the kitchen, pulled up the rug on the floor, and opened a trap door. Sending his wife down first, he turned just before the trap door was to close and looked at Jake, whispering, "I'm sorry Mr. Sullivan. Good luck."

Jake nodded as the trap door closed behind him. Then Lou put the rug back over it. Mike motioned once again for them to wait and took out his phone. Punching in the number Adams had given him, he sent him a message.

"Captured by Vaughan. Too much fire power. Burkes escaped in the jungle in the back of the house – have the evidence. Call Bates. Tracking information with Burkes."

"That should do it," said Mike, looking at Jake and Lou, who nodded their heads in affirmation.

Mike looked at Lou. "You got any idea where they'll take us?"

"Closest place to get off the island from here is the Bitter End Yacht Club. I'm sure someone like Hamilton has a slip or two there where he moors his yacht or yachts. I'm thinking that's where we'll be headed."

"If they don't kill us en route," said Jake.

Mike nodded his head, looked at Lou and Jake, and said, "Let's do this. All right Vaughan!" he called. "You win! We're coming out! We have the ledger! Just give me your word you'll let the Burkes go unharmed!"

"You three come out with the ledger . . . you have my word! Leave your weapons there!" called Vaughan. "Come out. . . hands where I can see them!"

With that, the three men headed for the door.

CHAPTER 38

Dusk was settling in as the three men emerged onto the porch and made their way down the steps, stopping in front of Vaughan and his men.

"Wise decision, gentlemen."

He motioned for the men to approach as he took the ledger and file from Jake. They bound each of the three men's hands behind their backs with plastic cuffs and then moved back behind Vaughan. Vaughan smiled.

"The famous Jake Sullivan and Mike Lang. You, I know. But you . . ." he said approaching Lou. "Who the hell are you?"

"Me? I'm just a bartender," said Lou.

Vaughan laughed. "Maybe now, but not before."

Lou stared into Vaughan's dead eyes. "Yeah, you're right. Before . . . I spent a lot of time taking care of assholes like you."

"Is that right?" chuckled Vaughan, as he walked around behind Lou. "So you were one of the self-described good guys? Well, sorry . . . I'm not." And with that, he drove the butt of the automatic weapon he held into Lou's kidneys, sending him to his knees.

"All right!" said Jake. "Enough! We did what you asked! We're here! Let's get on with this."

"Don't be in a hurry, Mr. Sullivan," said Vaughan, turning so they were face-to-face. "My employer's waiting to meet you."

"Looking forward to it," said Jake.

"I don't think you are, Mr. Sullivan . . . I don't think you are."

Vaughan motioned for two of his men to take them, and they headed down the hill toward the car. Talking to the other two men, he said, "Take a vehicle and go secure the dock. We'll meet you there." Stopping just below the crest, where they could still make out the house, Vaughan motioned to one of the men.

"All right, we're far enough away. Light it up!"

And with that, the man put the RPG on his shoulder and pulled the trigger, while Jake screamed, "Vaughan, you bastard! You promised!"

"Yeah, well like I said, I'm one of the bad guys."

The house went up in a fireball, the explosion shaking the ground they were on, debris flying in all directions. Nodding in satisfaction, Vaughan looked at the three and smiled, "Let's get a move on, gentlemen. We have an appointment to keep." Then his men began pushing the three down the hill to where the cars were parked.

When they came to the Range Rover and saw it, it was Lou who spoke.

"Son of a bitch . . . so that's how you did it."

Vaughan looked at him and smiled. "I figured you'd recognize it. Nice equipment, huh?"

"What is it?" said Mike.

"That clear antenna on top of the Rover . . . a sound receiver. That's how they picked up what we were saying in the house. I couldn't figure out how you were able to bug it when you didn't know where it was. You needed us to lead you to it."

"Very good, counselor, very good. You figured it out. Now please, get in the vehicle and we'll be on our way."

Vaughan then directed one of the "policemen" to ride on the jump seat in the rear with Jake, Mike, and Lou and another to drive, while he took the front passenger seat, and they headed out onto North Sound Road.

CHAPTER 39

Bill Adams was still several miles from the cutoff at Soldier Bay when the ground shook with an explosion and he saw a fireball and smoke rising above the trees ahead of him. Just then his phone beeped and he stopped. He saw the text from Mike.

Hitting the gas, he drove until he found the cutoff and then headed up the drive as quickly as he could and parked his vehicle in front of the ruins that were once the home of Mrs. Burke's sister.

Sidestepping the debris, gun drawn just in case any of Vaughan's men had stayed behind, he moved carefully around to what once was the back of the house, and moved into the jungle.

Having gone some distance, he stopped and began retracing his steps when he caught a glimpse of color and movement off to his right. Leveling his weapon at the spot, he called out, "Mr. and Mrs. Burke! It's Bill Adams, FBI! If that's you, come out with your hands up!"

Slowly Mr. and Mrs. Burke emerged from their hiding spot, Mrs. Burke clinging to the ledger and files, Mr. Burke's upraised right hand still holding his rifle.

"Drop the rifle, Mr. Burke," said Adams.

Burke complied. "I have a message for you from Jake Sullivan," said Burke.

"I'm sure you do," said Adams, motioning with the gun, he said, "now move out here onto the path. Now, Mrs. Burke, come to me slowly and give me the documents."

She complied, handing the paperwork to Adams, her hands shaking so badly she almost dropped them.

Adams scanned through the paperwork and stopped when he came to one of the last pages in the ledger.

"This last series of payments, what are they?"

"I'm not sure. What that amounts to is Hamilton distributing almost half of his empire to someone or something . . . codename 'Tiberius'. There was supposed to be one final entry this coming week, which would have given a controlling interest to that entity."

"Shit!" said Adams under his breath.

"What is it?" said Burke.

"You don't want to know."

Looking back at Mrs. Burke, who was still visibly shaken, Adams said, "It will be all right, Mrs. Burke. Just calm down. You have to understand, I have to take precautions here. Now, both of you, please sit down here on the path, cross your legs, and put your hands interlocked behind your head. Alright, Mr. Burke, start talking. Tell me what I have and what happened here."

The Burkes then told Adams everything that happened, including every detail they could think of.

"Mr. Lang said I'm supposed to give you this. It's a tracking device. It'll let you find them," handing over the wristband Mike had given him. "And you have the ledger and the documents, and they'll prove what I've told you."

Adams looked at them long and hard and made his decision. Holstering his weapon, he told them, "All right, I buy your story, folks, but you have to tell this to someone else, and to do that, I have to get you out of here. Hold on while I make a call."

Next Adams punched out one of the numbers Mike had given him into his phone. He was wondering if Jason Bates worked on a Monday night when he got his answer.

"This is Bates."

"Mr. Bates, this is Bill Adams with the FBI."

"Why are you calling, Mr. Adams? Why aren't you calling your supervisor or the Director?"

"Mr. Bates, I hate to be blunt, but I'm gonna ask you to be quiet and listen. Jake Sullivan and Mike Lang and another gentleman who's been helping them have just been captured by a mercenary in the employ of Hamilton Industries by the name of Aiden Vaughan. You can check him out on Interpol. He's a mercenary and assassin for hire. Before they were captured, they obtained new information from the two witnesses who had testified that they saw Jake leaving the crime scene. These two were coerced into making false statements against Jake by Vaughan and his employer, Adolphus Hamilton, in exchange for saving the life of their daughter, who has a serious medical condition, and because they were in fear for their own lives. Mr. Burke was an accountant for Hamilton and kept a ledger of his illegal activities, along with files documenting certain transactions and scientific matters dealing with the oil industry. Those documents are now in my possession.

I fully believe that Jake Sullivan is innocent and I'm not sure why he was chosen for this frame-up, but it has to do with the independence movement here in the islands and cornering the market on oil distribution around the world. And one other thing, I need you to run financials. I think we have a major problem," and Adams explained his fears to Jason Bates.

"Mr. Adams, I thank you for the information. Earlier this evening, I received information which corroborates what you have told me and clearly supports your conclusion of Jake's innocence. However, if the information you described means what you think it does, we have a much larger problem that we have to deal with. I am currently preparing to head to the Virgin Islands. Additionally, I have directed the USS Carney, now in transit from Puerto Rico, to head to St. Croix. The Carney has a Navy Seal team on board that is working with the DEA on drug interdiction in the Caribbean. The destroyer is equipped with a helipad. Might you have access to a helicopter, Mr. Adams?"

Looking at the Burkes, Adams smiled. "I think I know where you're going with this, Mr. Bates, and believe it or not, I actually do."

"Splendid," said Bates. "I suggest you make the necessary arrangements to obtain safe passage for Mr. and Mrs. Burke to the USS Carney as quickly as possible, along with the documents you have mentioned. Have your pilot contact Commander Morton on the flight deck once he has visual confirmation and all arrangements will be made for his safe landing."

"One request, Mr. Bates," said Adams.

"What would that be?" said Bates.

"Once the Burkes and the documents are safely delivered, my pilot, who shall remain nameless, is free to immediately take off without being followed or tracked."

"I take it that it would be best if we leave out the exact nature of your relationship with this pilot . . . yes, Mr. Adams?"

"Absolutely," said Adams.

"You have my word," said Bates.

"Well, let me get to it, Mr. Bates. Hopefully, I'll see you later tonight."

"How so?" said Bates.

"I'm going after them, sir, to try and stop them. But before I do, I have some tracking codes to give you that'll lead you and the Seal team to Jake if I'm unsuccessful."

There was silence for a few moments, then Bates spoke.

"Mr. Adams, I thank you for your service, as I am sure does the President of the United States, with whom I am about to discuss these matters. Good luck to you, and God's speed."

"Thank you, Mr. Bates. Now, here are the coordinates."

When he was done, Adams clicked off the phone and headed to his vehicle.

Passing the Burkes, he stopped. "You two are going to be safe. That man I was talking to was Jason Bates."

"He works for the President, doesn't he?" said Mr. Burke.

"Exactly. Look, it's a political situation that I can't get into, but Bates needs this evidence before the government can lend a hand to Jake and Mike, and you're going to deliver it to him."

"What about our part with the Bollinger murder and what happened to Mr. Sullivan?" said Mr. Burke.

"I think we will be able to work it out. You were threatened and you were coerced. I can't tell you that you are going to walk away scot-free, but we'll do what we can. Your efforts here warrant that consideration. I have to go. I have to find Mike and Jake and do what I can to help them. Move up to the front of the house and wait there, out of sight. A guy named Snake is coming to pick you up. He's okay. Go with him. He's going to put you on a helicopter and take you to a US Naval destroyer heading this way. You'll be taken into protective custody, and you'll be safe. When you get there, tell the people in charge about your daughter and the rest of your family in St. Louis, and we'll make sure they're protected, also."

Burke stood up and extended his hand. "I can't ask for more, Mr. Adams. I'm sorry for what I've done, but we couldn't let our daughter die."

"I understand," said Adams. "Just stay out of sight up there as best you can until Snake gets here. After what they did to this house, they think you're dead. No one's going to come back looking. Now I've gotta go. Good luck."

Reaching his car, he got in and turned on the ignition, then looked at the wristband he was wearing. The blip was still. He checked the coordinates.

"Gun Creek," he said to himself. "They're getting ready to head to the Bitter End . . . take a yacht out. I still have time."

He then hit a number into his phone. It was time to talk to Snake.

Snake was a good guy. He'd flown in Dessert Storm. He spent his time in the service ferrying munitions from supply ships in the Gulf to troops heading toward Baghdad. Somehow one of the cartels found out about his talents and wanted to employ him . . . island hopping . . . delivering drugs . . . and he came to the FBI asking for help. Bill had stuck out his neck for him and staged an elaborate, very public arrest, and the cartel backed off, not wanting to do business with anyone who was on the radar with the FBI.

"Snake . . . Bill Adams. Listen . . . how'd you like to do a little night-time landing on a Navy destroyer?"

"Hell yes, man!" came the reply. "I haven't done that shit since the war."

"Listen, I've got two very scared, very good people that I've got to get off the island and into protective custody. They're up here near Soldier Bay. How long from where you are in Spanish Town?"

"Get the chopper up and running . . . check everything out . . . less than an hour in the Rover."

"All right, here's the thing. The USS Carney is heading to St. Croix from Puerto Rico. Once you have a visual, call in to Commander Morton on the flight deck. He'll direct your landing. Once these two folks are safe on board, you take off . . . no questions asked. Deal?"

"Bill, I owe you. You got it."

"All right, Snake, here's where you'll find them," and Bill gave him the information on where Mrs. Burke's sister's house used to stand.

CHAPTER 40

On the drive to Gun Creek, Vaughan, sitting in the front passenger seat, with one of the officers driving and another guarding Jake, Mike, and Lou, placed a call.

"It's Vaughan. I have the three of them, and the other problem has been taken care of. We're on our way to Gun Creek. We're going to take the ferry over to the Bitter End and get the Hamilton yacht. No, it's too late, the airport's closed, and with the men and equipment we have, I think we'd be less conspicuous on the water. There's not much wind tonight. We should be able to make it by 11:00. Right. I'll let you know when we're getting close."

In the back, Jake said, "Say hello to Hamilton for me."

"Yes, sir." Vaughan clicked off and turned around and stared at Jake. "Think you have everything all figured out don't you, Mr. Sullivan? By the way . . . what's that on your arm?"

"Just a cut. Nothing to worry about," said Jake.

"Really? Let's have a look."

Vaughan climbed back and sat on the unoccupied jump seat – the other jump seat, holding the guard, who kept his weapon trained on the three. Pulling Jake forward, Vaughan unwrapped the bandage on his left arm.

"Looks pretty superficial, Mr. Sullivan. Maybe something just under the skin?"

And with that, he pulled out a knife, put the tip in the wound, and probed. Jake's reflex was to pull his arm back, but Vaughan's hold was like a vice. Jake refused to cry out and gritted his teeth.

"Ah, I think we have it," said Vaughan, and he pushed the edges of the wound together and popped the end of the capsule that Mike had implanted in Jake's arm. "Well, what do you know? Looks like a tracking device to me. Nice planning, boys."

Vaughan looked out the front window and saw an older man on a bicycle coming from the other direction, baskets over the rear wheels. Tapping the driver on the shoulder, he said, "Get him to stop and pull over. Ask him for directions."

The driver rolled down his window and flagged down the bicycle, and Vaughan opened the door and got out.

"My friend, can you tell me, is this the way to Gun Creek?"

"It is. About two miles ahead. Just stay on this road . . . that's all you have to do," said the man.

Vaughan put out his hand to thank him, and when he did so with his left hand, he dropped the tracking device in the baskets on the bicycle. Walking up to the rear door to close it, he looked in and saw the bandage that had been wrapped around Jake's wound lying on the floor. He picked it up and threw it at Mike.

"Here! You better re-wrap your friend's arm before he bleeds to death." Looking at Jake, he said, "I hope that hurts like hell." He shut the door and got back in the front passenger's seat.

Arriving at the Customs House and ferry terminal, Vaughan was happy to see that there were only a few boats making entry into North Sound and only one couple waiting for the ferry to go over to the Bitter End. His men had arrived and were on the dock with their gear. Forcing Jake, Mike, and Lou to sit on the dock, he told the two police officers who had accompanied him to guard them and posted his other men to watch all points of entry.

Unknown to Vaughan or anyone else, Lou had been working on the edge of his seat belt trying to cut through the plastic zip tie holding his hands behind his back. They arrived before he had finished the job, but he believed that if he yanked with sufficient strength, they would break. The question was when.

Just then, Vaughan saw the lights of the ferry approaching and picked up Jake just as it reached the dock.

"My name is Thomas Dalton," he said to the ferry manager as he approached. "I'm chief of security with Hamilton Industries. These four men are with the U.S.V.I. Police Department. This is a fugitive we have apprehended. We're taking him to the Bitter End for transport, and we need to use the ferry, and we need you to cast off now. You understand, we need to do this . . ." and Vaughan's words were cut off when Bill Adams came around the corner of The Last Stop bar.

"FBI! Drop your weapons and hands in the air!"

Adams had his gun on Vaughan, who moved Jake in front of him and put a gun to his head.

"That's not going to happen."

"Take your shot Bill!" yelled Jake. "They need me alive! He's not going to shoot me!"

"Bill, is it? You want to take that chance with me?"

Out of the corner of his eye, Bill saw one of the police officers going for his gun. He swiveled, dropped into firing position, and fired and dropped him to the deck. In that instant, Lou strained his arms as best he could and the plastic cuff snapped. He swung his legs out, knocking the legs out from under the guard standing almost on top of him. The guard on the other side drew his gun. Lou rolled, grabbed the guard who had fallen, and sat him up in front of him, picking up his fallen gun at the same time. The guard fired, hitting the guard in front of Lou, and Lou returned fire, taking out the guard. The one guard remaining had dropped to the deck, getting off several shots in Adams's direction, but Adams fired back, and he went silent.

During the midst of the action, Vaughan trained the gun on the ferry operator.

"Get us out of here, across to the Bitter End as fast as you can! Move!" Pointing to the young couple who had been waiting for the ferry, Vaughan said, "Get on here now!" Pointing the gun directly at them, he said, "You heard me! Get on here now!"

They did as they were told.

"Each of you . . . take a seat in the back, and don't move. Let's go! Get this thing up to speed!" he said to the ferry operator, as they started out into the Sound. He had hoped the young couple would give some cover and make those on the shore afraid to shoot. It looked like his men were losing the battle, and his obligation was to bring in Sullivan. They were expendable.

Lou sat up and looked around. "Mike . . . you all right?"

Mike had tried to get up to run into the one guard beside him, but the guard had hit him on the back of the neck with his gun before turning on Adams. Stunned, Mike was kneeling on the dock.

"Yeah, I'm fine. See how Bill is."

Lou went over to where Adams was, sitting with his back against The Last Stop bar, his legs sprawled and his arms down behind him, his right one still holding the gun. Lou reached down and in the light on the dock, saw the dark spreading stain on his chest. Lowering his head, he muttered, "Son of a bitch. Hold on Bill, we're gonna get you some help."

With his last bit of strength, Adams grabbed Lou's shirt and pulled him closer. Lou bent into him and listened . . . and then came the death rattle . . . and he was gone.

Lou came walking back toward Mike, who was standing upright now but still shaking off the cobwebs.

"How is he?" said Mike, looking up. As soon as he saw Lou's face, he knew. "No . . . no," said Mike, and he went running over to Bill, hands still cuffed behind his back, and knelt down.

Lou came over and put a hand on Mike's shoulder. "Come on, Mike. You can't help him now. We have to move. Vaughan's taken Jake and we need to get after him."

"You don't understand," said Mike, looking up at Lou. "I did this to him. I got him involved in this, and now he's dead."

"Mike, I know he was your friend, but that's bullshit. He was FBI. He had a job to do, and he was doing it. He was a good man, and he died doing what he had to do. You can't blame yourself for that." And with that, he turned Mike around. Having gotten a knife from one of Vaughan's men, he cut through the plastic, releasing the cuffs.

Mike turned around and looked at Lou, rubbing his wrists to bring back the circulation. "The hell I can't," he said. Then he started walking toward the dead bodies. "Let's empty one of the duffle bags, get some weapons and some ammo, and go after this son of a bitch." Looking back at Lou, he said, "It's personal for both of us now."

"Amen brother," said Lou. "Let's go get him." And he and Mike checked the bodies for guns and ammunition, took what they could, and put it in the duffle bag.

Lou stopped what he was doing for a minute and looked at Mike. "Does the word 'Tiberius' mean anything to you, Mike?"

Looking up, Mike said, "No, why?"

"I swear that was the last thing Adams said to me before he died."

"Tiberius? Like the Roman emperor?" said Mike.

"Yeah. I don't know whether it's code for something . . . I don't get it."

Mike shook his head. "Doesn't mean anything to me. I don't know. You sure that's what he was saying?"

"I don't know, Mike. It was with his last breath. Maybe I heard it wrong. We better get moving."

The people that had been hiding in the Custom House and the bar had come out. Lou walked up to them, causing them all to cower back.

"Police business. Nothing to worry about. Best you get back inside, though," which they quickly did.

Just then, another boat was coming in to the dock. A small black man in shorts and a t-shirt was just tying up when Lou came over.

"Out fishing tonight, sir?"

"A little said the man," looking at Lou. "Can I help you?"

"Yes you can. I need your boat."

"What?"

Lou raised the gun he had been holding at his side. "I'm sorry. It's a matter of life and death. Police business. Hope you understand, now get out of the boat."

Mike had come up behind him and threw the duffle bag in the boat, reached in, and helped the startled man out.

"But you can't take my boat."

"I'm afraid we have to. I'm sorry. You'll find it over at the Bitter End"

And with that, Lou got into the boat after Mike, untied the bow line, and started the outboard, and they headed out across the Sound to the Bitter End.

CHAPTER 41

As Mike and Lou headed across the North Sound, the ferry had already docked at the Bitter End. Vaughan pointed a gun at the ferry operator and the two passengers.

"You all stay here for fifteen minutes and don't move. My men are watching this boat, and if you do . . . well, you can imagine."

And with that, he pushed the gun into Jake's spine and pushed him off the ferry onto the dock.

"Not a sound," said Vaughan. They encountered few people as they made their way to the slip where the Hamilton Industries yacht was berthed. Pushing Jake up the gangplank, Vaughan shouted, "Captain!" Once again, with much more emphasis, "Captain!" The captain appeared, rubbing his eyes, buttoning his shirt.

"Mr. Dalton? What is it?"

Pushing Jake down into one of the seats, he barked at the captain, "Get us out to sea as fast and as quietly as you can. I want as little attention as possible."

Hurrying to the helm, the Captain, knowing Dalton's reputation, had only one question.

"What's the destination, Mr. Dalton?"

"St. Croix. Krause Lagoone. As fast as you can, within legal limits as soon as we hit open water."

Walking toward the bar, he asked over his shoulder, "Anyone else on board?"

"No, sir."

"Good," said Dalton, as he poured himself two fingers of scotch into a crystal tumbler and then sat down opposite Jake. "I'd offer you a drink, Mr. Sullivan, but I understand you're a teetotaler these days."

Jake just stared, refusing to play his game.

"Don't feel like conversation, huh? Just as well." Downing the drink in one swallow, Vaughan set the glass on the end table beside him. "I'm going to lean my head back and close my eyes, Mr. Sullivan. I need a little rest . . . but be assured, the slightest movement from you, and I will be wide awake. So just enjoy the ride and don't try anything."

Jake leaned his head back and closed his eyes. "Even though the day's been uneventful, I could use a little sleep myself," said Jake.

"Ever laughing in the face of danger, hey Sullivan?" said Vaughan.

"Something like that," said Jake.

Then silence descended upon the cabin – the only sound the throbbing of the engines, and the waves lapping against the hull as the yacht moved forward.

CHAPTER 42

Lou watched Mike hold an object up into the night sky, trying to get a better reading.

"Is that what I think it is?" said Lou.

"Yeah, I took it off Bill Adams's wrist."

"Have you picked them up?"

"Yeah. Looks like they're heading out to sea through the entrance to the Sound."

"I told you that plan would work," said Lou. "Vaughan fell for it. That fake we put in Jake's arm was the sugar – the placebo. Once he saw that, he wouldn't look any further for the real deal."

"I just gotta figure out how we get a boat when we get there," said Mike.

"No problem," said Lou. "Mine's there and waiting for us."

"What?" said Mike.

"I had one of my friends bring it over. I had a feeling things might end up here and it might be needed . . . and I know the bartender at the Club House. He looks after things for me."

"You know Lou, you saw what happened back there. I can't ask you for more than you've already done. If you want to get out, I understand."

"Hell Mike . . . I'm just getting started. Two good men are dead . . . probably more . . . I'm in it to the end." He slid the boat into a berth and tied up at the Bitter End. "Follow me," said Lou, and they trotted to the slip where Lou's boat was moored.

Reaching under the steering column, Lou found the keys where he had told his friend to hide them, started up the boat, and headed out.

Mike had stowed their gear and they were on their way, heading out of North Sound, past Vixen Point on Prickly Pear Island and on Mosquito Island they saw the lights of Drake's Anchorage on the left, swung around into open waters, and headed into the Sir Francis Drake Channel.

"The reading shows he's dead ahead of us," said Mike, "about five hundred yards."

"Must be those lights up there," said Lou. "We'll hang back and follow them."

"Where do you think they're headed?" asked Mike.

"Given everything that we learned from the Burkes, I think we're going to the center of this whole thing . . . the old refinery on St. Croix. So settle back my friend," said Lou, "we're going to be on the water for a couple hours, give or take."

"You have enough fuel?" said Mike.

"No problem. Specially made . . . just in case."

"Naturally," said Mike.

"Don't worry," said Lou. "We'll get there. And when we do, we're going to end this once and for all."

Mike leaned back and looked at the night sky, full of stars sparkling like diamonds on black velvet and hoped that end would be as they planned.

CHAPTER 43

As soon as Vaughan had closed his eyes and several minutes had passed, Jake opened his and began to take note of the shoreline as they passed. Soon they would come to what he'd been waiting for. The yacht passed the lights of Spanish Town, and finally he could barely make out what he thought was the outcropping of the Baths. Looking over his shoulder at the captain, he decided to make his move.

Jumping up, he hit the captain with the full weight of his shoulder, turned and with the steering wheel behind him, turned it as far left as fast as he could, then pushed the throttle bar forward to full speed.

Dalton, true to his word, was up and moving after Jake and grabbed him to move him away, but Jake held on to the steering wheel, keeping it turned to the left, the yacht heading for shore with ever-increasing speed.

Vaughan kneed Jake in the midsection, causing him to release his grip, and threw him to the ground, frantically turning the steering wheel hard right and pulling back the throttle to stop, but it was too late. The yacht's hull ground against the bottom as it slammed into the shore, knocking the captain who had been trying to get up back off his feet, and Vaughan fell on top of him. Getting back his breath after Dalton's blow, Jake raced for the side and jumped overboard, landing in the shallow water. Righting himself, he splashed for the shore and headed for the rock formation known as the Baths.

The moon was bright and he finally found an entranceway into the rocks and headed in. He had two choices: head left and climb up a rope on the rocks to a wooden ladder system up above or take a passage to the right. But he realized he only had one choice – his hands were still cuffed behind his back, and there was no way he could climb. He headed toward the right. Finding a niche among the rocks, he stopped and listened. He heard the sound of footsteps in the cavern. "More than one," he thought. "The captain must be coming, too."

Suddenly there was silence, and then the sounds picked up again, but he couldn't quite make out whether there was one or two sets of footsteps he was hearing, growing nearer.

Moving out from the niche, he headed away from the footsteps and came out of the rocks into a clearing on the beach of a small bay. Looking around, he realized there was nowhere to go, so he simply sat down on the sand.

Soon, Vaughan clambered down from the rocks above him, having taken the upper route, and the captain exited the rocks the same way Jake had come. Vaughan roughly pulled him to his feet.

"Very cute, Mr. Sullivan. What do you think this has gotten you?"

"I don't know, but you're not getting that yacht off the sand and back out to sea, that's for sure . . . not tonight."

Vaughan threw Jake down onto the sand. "You're a fool Sullivan. You're only delaying the inevitable."

Dalton reached for his phone and began to enter a number to call for a boat when he heard a noise coming from the caverns. He quickly pulled out his gun, yanked up Jake, and stood him in front of him, holding the gun once again to his head. It was then that Mike and Lou burst from the cavern entrance, each holding a gun out in front of them.

CHAPTER 44

Mike had been dozing in the back of the boat, waking with a start every so often and checking the GPS, but this time he was awakened by Lou.

"Mike! Check that thing! Those lights just turned sharp left!"

Quickly Mike scanned the GPS. "Jake, what are you doing?" he said.

"They're heading in to shore. It looks like it's moving too quickly. Shit!" said Lou, "he's going to ground the yacht!"

"Can you tell where they are?"

"Yeah, we just passed Spanish Town. My guess is he picked the Baths. He must be going to try and hide out in the rocks."

"That crazy son of a bitch," said Mike. "Why couldn't he just ride this out?"

"It's not in his nature to go quietly," said Lou. "I can tell that much about him."

"You've got a point there," said Mike.

"There's the yacht up ahead. I'm going to go in," said Lou, and he turned the boat and headed for shore. Much farther out than the yacht, he threw the anchor in and moored the boat. Mike jumped into the shallow water and headed for shore, but Lou grabbed him.

"Stop and think for a second," said Lou. "They're going to need a boat. They're never going to get that yacht out. We still have to tie this thing to Hamilton, and that's where they're taking him."

"So what are you suggesting?" asked Mike.

"Let's give them a boat. We find Jake and we surrender, and he takes us all."

Taking his gun out of his waistband and checking it, Mike looked at Lou. "Sounds like a plan. Let's make this look good."

Lou followed Mike into the surf and they hit the beach running to the entrance of the rock formation, ready to burst out the other side.

CHAPTER 45

"All right, you two," said Dalton, "stop right there!"

"Do me a favor," said Jake, "kill this guy, will you?"

Vaughan yanked him closer. "I strongly suggest you don't try that, gentlemen. Even if you get me, my reflex will blow his head off."

Lou and Mike looked at each other and dropped their weapons.

"Captain . . . if you please."

The captain went over and took the guns from them.

"Well gentlemen, I must say . . . you couldn't have come at a better time. You've given me just what I need."

"What's that?" said Mike.

"Your boat."

Pushing Jake down to the sand, he lifted his gun and pointed it at Lou and Mike.

"Of course, I don't need you. The question is . . . do I kill you here or take you with me?"

"Your choice, pal," said Lou, "but unfortunately, I'm not real good on maintenance. The boat has a lot of problems. I can coax it along, but I don't know what's going to happen with you at the wheel."

"That's fine," said Vaughan, swinging the gun in Mike's direction, "but that doesn't stop me from killing him."

"Sorry . . . you kill him and you have to kill me too," said Lou.

Jake rolled away and stood up. "And me too."

Vaughan shook his head.

"I don't have time for this. Move! We're heading for your boat. I can always kill you later."

When they reached the shore on the other side of the rock formation, Vaughan told the captain to get back on the yacht and call for help and get it off the beach. He then waded out to Lou's boat with Mike and Lou in front of him, still holding Jake close to him with the gun at his head. Directing the three to stand there, he pulled himself over the side of the boat opposite them so he could keep his weapon trained on them, and then ordered them to climb into the boat, which they did, helping Jake on board.

Vaughan sat Mike and Jake opposite him so he could keep the gun on them and told Lou to head for St. Croix, giving him the coordinates.

"Make sure your lights are on, and get this thing going as fast as you can within the limits. I don't want to attract any attention. And don't try anything. Believe me, whatever you do, I can kill these two before you ever get to me."

"St. Croix it is," said Lou. "Any particular location?"

"The refinery at Krause Lagoone," said Vaughan.

"Just as I thought," said Lou to himself. "Just as I thought."

ST. CROIX

U.S.V.I.

CHAPTER 46

Vaughan had been right. It was just after 11:00 when Lou cut the engines and pulled into one of the refinery docks at Krause Lagoone. After tying up, Vaughan ordered Lou and Mike out and had them help Jake onto the dock and then told them to walk down the dock and stop. Once they were a sufficient distance away, he exited the boat onto the dock and followed behind them, giving them directions how to proceed.

"There's a light up ahead in that one bay. That's where we're going," he said. "Now move along."

Entering through the doorway, they found themselves in what looked like a loading zone – the chains still hung from overhead cranes and conveyor belts headed out toward the dock. Up ahead, a pan light hung from the ceiling, casting strange shadows on the machinery and equipment stacked against the walls covered in dust and cobwebs.

"Nice place you have here, Vaughan," said Mike.

"Enjoy it. It's the last place you'll ever see," said Vaughan.

"Now, keep moving."

As they approached the light, four armed men appeared from out of the shadows and sat down three metal chairs. One by one, Vaughan pushed Lou, Mike, and Jake each onto a chair.

Jake looked at Mike and shook his head.

"Again, the handcuffs ... the chair ... the light. You've gotta be kidding me."

Before Mike could respond, an older man appeared out of the shadows. Dressed in a perfectly tailored gray, chalk-striped suit, immaculate white shirt, tie and matching pocket hankie, with a perfectly-styled mane of white hair.

"The famous Jake Sullivan and Mike Lang," he said, "and, of course, Attorney Bassett."

"Actually, pal, I'm just a bartender," said Lou. His retort got him smacked on the back of his neck with the butt of an automatic weapon from one of the guards.

"You must be Hamilton," said Jake.

"That's right, Mr. Sullivan. I am. Adolphus Hamilton, to be exact."

"Well, you have me here ... now what do you want?"

"What do I want, Mr. Sullivan? I want revenge."

"For what? I've never met you in my life."

"No, but you did meet someone I held quite dear."

"The only person in the Virgin Islands I had any contact with was a young girl named Alaina Alvarez, and we checked her obituary. Her next of kin were her mother and father, and that was all that was listed. Surely if she was a relative of a great man such as yourself that fact would have been made known."

"It would have, had I not disowned her prior to her death."

"What?" said Mike.

"You see, my granddaughter was impetuous. She didn't like the lifestyle of these islands. She wanted to go to the big city in the United States and make a career for herself. I tried to explain to her that her place was here with her family ... with what I had built here for her. She refused ... so I cut her off. It was her impetuousness that got her killed. It was what I had warned her would happen in your Godforsaken country, but she wouldn't listen . . . and she paid the ultimate price."

"So what's this about?" said Mike. "Do you even care enough about your own granddaughter to mourn her death? What revenge do you want?"

Hamilton moved closer to Sullivan. "Due to you being a drunkard, Mr. Sullivan, and a failure, you let my granddaughter's killer go free."

"You're right. That's exactly what I was. But I caught Ortiz, and I made him pay the ultimate price, and Mike and I caught the man who owned him, and we did the same to him. What more do you want?"

"Too late, Mr. Sullivan . . . too late. Do you remember coming out of the courtroom, Mr. Sullivan, after your inept appearance? The judge had thrown out all charges, including my granddaughter's murder. Do you remember looking into the eyes of her mother and father?"

"The eyes," thought Jake, "the eyes. The portrait in your office . . . that was . . ."

"Yes, Mr. Sullivan. That was my daughter. That was my daughter who two weeks after the trial, consumed by grief – there was no justice for her daughter – hung herself."

Jake looked down and shook his head. "I'm sorry. I didn't know."

Livid with rage and hatred, Hamilton almost shrieked. "I don't want your sympathies Sullivan! I want your death! Since my wife died in Maria's childbirth, she was the only thing I had. She was the only thing I've loved. She was my world . . . and you took her away from me! And I will see you dead for it!"

"Wait," said Mike. "Your hatred of Jake is one thing. Why try to set him up as a murderer?"

"So the world could see the kind of man he truly is . . . not the great hero he's portrayed to be! This man who is the right hand to the President of the United States, who solves crimes no one else can, who brings to justice those who no one else can, who finds fortunes supposedly lost, stops wars . . . I want them to see him for what he really is!"

"So all this was just your hatred? That's all?"

A voice spoke out from the dark. "Not quite, Mr. Lang. Not quite. You see, Mr. Hamilton isn't the director of the drama. He's only a player."

And out of the shadows walked Arthur Braxton, U.S. Attorney for the Virgin Islands, holding the ledger and the other documents.

"No . . . I'm afraid the director's chair belongs to me."

"Art . . . What?"

"C'mon Jake. Don't be so surprised."

"But why?"

"Why? Why do you think? Power, fame, fortune, and sadly to say, a little jealousy. The mighty Jake Sullivan brought to his knees. You always stayed one step ahead of me, Jake. You always got the notoriety, the plum positions . . . but now here we are. You – about to die, and me – about to become the first President of the Independent Virgin Islands. Oh, and might I add . . . a majority shareholder of Hamilton Industries, with all the wealth we are about to accumulate through my partner's wonderful new technologies in gas and oil." Looking at Jake, he said, "Not bad for a black kid from the slums of St. George Village on an island in the Caribbean, hey Jake?"

"Son of a bitch," said Lou.

"Ah, the bartender speaks."

Jake just looked at the floor and shook his head.

"What's the matter, Jake? Can't quite grasp it? It's really quite simple. I planned to indict Mr. Hamilton on all the things that are in this ledger which you so kindly led us to. But as I thought about it, I thought it might be better to strike a deal, so I approached Adolphus and told him I'd let him live as a free man if he turned over control of his company to me. Well, Adolphus is a proud man, and he said no, he'd rather take his chances and fight me in court. He told me of the great plans he had for these islands and he told me the one obstacle that stood in his way."

"Andre Bollinger," said Mike.

"Exactly. Too much of a radical past. Never would have been accepted by the world community. And that's even if he could have won. And then I got a notice one day – the famous Jake Sullivan was coming to our humble islands to speak at a Bench-Bar Conference. And it's as if fate herself had smiled upon me. That was the leverage I needed. That was the one thing I could give Adolphus that he wanted more than anything else – revenge against you. When I explained to him it would also take out our main opposition, he saw the wisdom of accepting my proposal."

"What happens to Donaldson?" asked Jake.

"Oh, he'll run . . . and he'll be elected Governor. He already knows that. But his term will be limited . . . and he'll be famous as the last Governor of the United States Territory of the Virgin Islands, because he will immediately ask for a referendum on independence from the United States. And with Adolphus's financial backing and my political clout, there is no doubt that will succeed. Mr. Hamilton's Republican Party will then nominate me for the first President of the Independent Virgin Islands. The PIVI have already agreed to my demands. And the rest, as they say, will be history."

"Art, you're in a little over your head, aren't you? What political clout do you have?"

"You'd be amazed, Jake. You know, I said I was going to get a little revenge here, too? You didn't help me any Jake when you took out my boss."

Jake looked long and hard at Braxton. "You were working for Matthews."

"Jake, there were more of us working for Matthews than you could ever imagine. Now, true, when you took out Matthews, the whole thing collapsed, but those ties that were formed still remain . . . and there are still people I can call upon . . . people of power, of influence, of wealth. The same people who were going to help make Benjamin Matthews President of the United States will have a much easier time making me President of a little island nation."

Footsteps were heard coming from the entry to the factory floor, and into the light strode none other than Jason Bates.

"I'll take that as a confession, Mr. Braxton. On behalf of the President of the United States, I hereby charge you, Arthur Tiberius Braxton, with high crimes and misdemeanors, including treason, conspiracy to commit murder, murder, and assorted other crimes we'll list in the paperwork."

As he finished talking, there silently appeared all around the room men in black combat gear, automatic rifles aimed at Hamilton, Braxton, Vaughan, and the four guards.

"I suggest you drop your weapons, gentlemen. These boys seldom miss."

As the Seal team came into view, Vaughan, knowing a disadvantage when he saw one, slinked back into the shadows. Lou, sitting closest to those shadows, moved quickly in the same direction. There was a continuous firepit to Braxton's right, burning off the oil vapors as they arose from the tank, into which Braxton flung the ledger.

"There is no confession, Mr. Bates, just me espousing my political ambitions. I'm sorry that my business partner here is guilty of

such despicable crimes against these men. I'll be happy to prosecute him to the fullest extent of the law."

By now, the Seals had disarmed the guards and had taken
Hamilton into custody.

"You lying bastard!" he said, straining to get away from the
Seals. I knew I was making a deal with the Devil."

"I'm sorry Adolphus. I'm afraid your lust for revenge has
clouded your faculties. I have no idea what you're talking about,
and I doubt," looking toward the fire, "that there's any paperwork
that substantiates any of the claims you are making."

Just then Bates held out one of his hands to one of the Seals,
taking the documents he provided. "Well, there is the copy that we
have, Arthur," said Bates. "I think it will be enough."

Braxton looked on in shock. "But Vaughan destroyed . . ."

"He destroyed one of the copies. But Mr. Burke had the fore-
sight to make two."

The Seals released Jake. Just then there was a clatter on the steel
steps, and soon Lou appeared, dragging Vaughan. He threw him
down on the floor at the feet of one of the Seals and looked at Bates.

"I thought you might want this guy. I think he's pretty nasty . .
. you know . . . murder, war crimes, things like that." Smiling at the
Seal, he put his fist to his chest. "Ready to Lead, Ready to Follow,
Never Quit."

The Seal smiled back and returned the salute, and Lou then
went back and sat down in his seat.

Vaughan sat up, blood coming from a gash on his cheek, his
nose obviously broken, and stared at Lou, who said, "You lose bad
guy!"

Jake walked up until he was face-to-face with Braxton, whose
smug expression was now deteriorating into one of fear of the
unknown.

"You know, Art, sometimes I'm not very good at the law, but it seems to me that . . . and Jason, correct me if I'm wrong . . . part of your crime was stealing the knife out of my office in Miami – the knife that became a murder weapon. So I think I get to try you for murder in federal court in Miami. Let's see how you like the cell, Arthur. See how you like it as the evidence mounts up. Only this time, you and I both know the murder charges are true . . . and we both know that I'm gonna win."

Just then, another Seal appeared, and marching in front of him was none-other than Commander Armand Lucien.

"This guy had docked a boat and was heading in here when I intercepted him, sir."

"And who might you be?" said Bates.

"I am Armand Lucien, Zone Commander of the United States Virgin Island Police Department on the island of St. John. I had heard word that Mr. Sullivan had been captured by parties unknown and was being held here. I came to ensure his safety."

Jake got up and walked over to Lucien.

"You're not even a good liar, Lucien. Jason . . ."he said to Bates, "meet the man who killed Andre Bollinger."

"How dare you!" said Lucien.

"Lucien, it's over. Quit your whining and for once be a man," said Vaughan.

"Quiet!" snapped Jake. "You see Lucien, I remember. I remember that white flutter I saw when Vaughan knocked me out on the path to the beach . . . at least I assume it was Vaughan. That white flutter I saw . . . that was you wiping your hands with your handkerchief. You're a germ-a-phobe . . . you do it all the time. You were there with the body that night, and you were in charge. That makes you a murderer."

"You have no proof!" said Lucien. "It's a lie!"

"I told you when I gave you the knife," said Vaughan, "and you wiped off your hands, 'old habits die hard'," and he started to laugh.

"You should've listened to me in that cell, Lucien. Remember what I told you? I told you I was going to get to the bottom of this, and when I did I was going to destroy everyone involved. You should've known I was talking about you." He looked at the Seal. "Get this piece of scum out of here!"

"Wait!" said Lucien as he was walked away. "You have no right! Wait . . . please! I can tell you things!"

Lucien's protestations finally drowned out as he was hauled outside. Bates then spoke to the Seal team commander.

"There's a transport waiting at the airport. Get these men in the vans and take them there. They're flying to Miami tonight."

"You can't do that," said Braxton.

"Oh, I can," said Bates. "Seeing as we have federal reciprocity with the Virgin Islands, and seeing how I've already called Judge Ashby and received a verbal order allowing extradition, I certainly can. Take them away men."

As the Seals took the men away, Jake turned to Jason.

"Nice timing."

"You do understand why we couldn't get into this sooner?" asked Bates.

"Oh, yeah, he understands," said Mike. "He's been chased all over the Virgin Islands, people were going to kill him after he was sent to prison – people were trying to kill him after he escaped – all because we didn't want to create a bad political issue for the President of the United States."

Bates looked down. "Jake, you do understand, don't you?"

"It's okay, Jason. I get it."

"And by the way, Jason," said Mike, "you told me you needed evidence before you could act. What evidence did you get?"

Bates put his head down again. "I understand Bill Adams died tonight. Is that true?"

"He did," said Mike. "He died saving us."

"So I understand," said Bates. "Well, he saved you in more ways than one. First, he saved Mr. and Mrs. Burke and got a friend of his to fly them to a Naval destroyer at my direction after he called me to make sure I would get the ledger and documents. You also need to thank your secretary. She sent me the photograph, as you suggested, which clearly proved your innocence. It was awfully hard of Jake to have mailed a murder weapon to Caneel Bay several days beforehand when it was still in his office on the day he left. That was all the proof we needed, given the fact that we knew Jake was innocent all along."

"Thanks for the vote of confidence, Bates," laughed Jake.

"Not just mine, Jake. The President of the United States wants you to know that he always believed in your innocence. And Mike, he always believed you would prove it. Listen, I have to get back. It appears there's some world economic problems that are going to arise we have to deal with concerning the oil market, but I think you boys deserve a vacation. You're here in paradise. Take some time off."

And with that, Bates turned and followed the Seals and their prisoners out of the factory.

"Jason!" called Jake after him. "How'd you know about Braxton?"

"The ledger . . . and the instincts of your friend, Mr. Adams. There were ledger entries at the very end of monies going to a source with the code word of 'Tiberius'. Mr. Burke told Adams there was enough transferred to give whomever that was half ownership of the company, with a final payment coming due this week that would have given that person a majority share. Mr. Adams recognized 'Tiberius' as Arthur Braxton's middle name. He figured that the final payment was what Braxton was going to get for turning you over to Hamilton, and he had me check out Braxton's financials . . . and he was right."

"So it was Braxton pulling the strings all along?"

"Appears that way," said Bates. "You should be honored, Jake. Hamilton hated you enough to give up everything he had just to be able to watch you die."

"Yeah, some honor," said Jake.

"Take care," said Bates, and he turned and went out.

Jake reached out and shook Mike's hand and clasped him on the shoulder.

"Mike, I don't know what to say."

"Hey, not that I'm keeping score," said Mike, "but I think I've saved you more than you've saved me."

"You know," said Jake, "you do this every time we get into one of these things. You're always keeping score about one thing or another."

"I'm just saying . . ."

Jake then held his hand out to Lou. "Lou, I gotta tell you . . . we couldn't have done this without you. Mike was right. You are one hell of a bartender."

"Always a pleasure," laughed Lou. "I love it when the good guys come out on top. Now let's go celebrate."

"Where to?" said Mike.

"Hey, my boat's still here. The night's still young. Soggy Dollar is still open, and if it isn't, I'll open it. You've still got your room at the Sand Castle . . . like the man said . . . take some time off. I think we need a party."

Mike looked at Jake. "Well?"

Jake started walking out the door. "I'm sure not going to argue with him."

And with that, they headed for Lou's boat.

EPILOGUE

JOST VAN DYKE

B.V.I.

CHAPTER 47

When they got back to the Soggy Dollar that night, Jake had had time to think, and he suggested to Lou and Mike that if they were going to celebrate, they should include other people. He put a call in to Bates and Bates agreed to his request. Placing several more calls, he made the necessary arrangements, and then the three headed off to get a good night's sleep.

Two days later, it was a beautiful day on the island of Jost Van Dyke. The winds were calm and the water sparkled in the sunlight.

Jake headed to the beach. He had just had a long phone conversation with Linda and the girls. He felt the same mixture of emotions he always did . . . love and remorse . . . hope and despair.

It was complicated. They all loved each other, but what had happened to Jake, and what they had to endure, stood in the way of being a family.

And it had happened to him again, and all he could do was reassure those he loved that he had once again survived.

He walked among the people on the beach and at the bar, shaking hands as he went. Lou's friend from MI6 was there and Lou had tracked down Snake, finding out who he was from some of his sources.

Jake thanked them both.

"I know I don't get to know who you really are," he said to the agent, and then looking at Snake, "and I know I don't want to know what you really do for a living . . . but I want to thank you both for all your help."

"Anything for Lou," said the agent. "Thank you, sir."

Jake laughed and turned. Walking away, he moved on to the happy couple sitting at the end of the bar.

"Mr. and Mrs. Burke . . ."

"Please, it's Marcus and Andrea," said Burke.

"All right, Marcus and Andrea . . . thank you for everything you did."

"Again, I apologize for how all this started," said Burke.

"All is forgiven. You were there when we needed you. That's what counts. By the way, how's your daughter doing?"

"She is responding to treatment and waiting for a donor match. Mr. Bates arranged a flight for us to St. Louis later today," said Andrea. "And we thank you for making sure that we're still here to be with our baby."

Next Jake moved on to a table and the Greek looked up from his book, his eyes still somewhat blackened from the meeting with Vaughan and his men Mike had predicted would come.

"My thanks, Greek," said Jake.

"A pleasure, Mr. Sullivan. It's always good to help the innocent."

"Innocent at least in this case," laughed Jake.

"We take our victories when we can, Mr. Sullivan. It was a pleasure."

"Sorry about the eye."

"Only a minor inconvenience. It will heal. It was sustained in a good cause."

"Thanks again."

Just then, Jake looked up to see Mike coming toward him, walking arm in arm with none other than Eva.

"Look who just arrived," said Mike.

Eva took off in a run and jumped into Jake's arms. Holding him close, she whispered, "I'm so glad you're safe. Why do you always have to scare the crap out of me?" she said, backing up and slapping him on the shoulder.

"Easy, Eva. Sorry. You know I bruise easily."

"You two drive me insane," she said looking at Mike and Jake. "But I love you both. Thank you for having me come here."

"You're always there for us, Eva," said Mike. "We appreciate it."

"More than you know," said Jake, toasting her with his glass of Diet Coke.

"Now if you two don't mind, I'm going over and talk to that nice, handsome bartender and get myself one of those famous Painkillers." And off she went.

They saw her as she reached the bar. She spoke to Lou, and he smiled and reached out and kissed her hand.

"This could be a problem," said Mike.

"Ah, let her have some fun. She's earned it. Well, my friend . . . you pulled it off. You got me out of it, just as you promised."

"Yeah. It worked out okay," said Mike. "It's like Lou said . . . you've gotta fight the bad guys, even though you lose people on the way."

"Yeah, said Jake," lifting his glass. "Here's to Bill Adams."

Mike lifted his drink as they stood and looked out at the boats bobbing up and down in the water. Just then, Lou approached. "And here's to Deke," and joined in the toast.

"Your secretary is one crazy lady," he said.

"Play nice," said Mike. "Don't forget . . . she's family."

"Easy brother . . . all's well."

Mike held out his hand. "Lou, again . . . thanks. We never could have pulled this off without you."

"Again, my pleasure my friend." Lou looked out over the water, too. "Beautiful day in paradise, isn't it?"

"Couldn't be better," said Jake.

Just then Mike's cell rang. "Excuse me a minute," and he turned to take the call.

"What? That's impossible!"

Jake and Lou looked toward Mike.

"All right, I got it," and he closed the phone, stood looking at the sand for a minute, then looked up at Jake and walked toward him. Jake knew the look.

"What is it, Mike?"

"They just found a murdered girl in South Beach – violated, mutilated, and a certain type of cross cut into each of her breasts."

"That can't be," said Jake.

"I'm afraid it is."

Lou shook his head. "Sorry boys. The monsters never sleep. Let's go get you packed."

With one last look at the beauty of the island and their friends and the people they'd met along the way, Jake and Mike turned to follow Lou. Vacation was over.

NEXT IN THE SERIES...

SON OF A SON OF A SAILOR
A JAKE SULLIVAN NOVEL
CHIP BELL
SON OF A SON OF A SAILOR
CHIP BELL

CHIP BELL

1725 FIFTH AVENUE
ARNOLD, PA 15068

724-339-2355

chip.bell.author@gmail.com
clb.bcymlaw@verizon.net
www.ChipBellAuthor.com

FOLLOW ME ON FACEBOOK
facebook.com/chipbellauthor

FOLLOW ME ON TWITTER
@ChipBellAuthor

FOLLOW ME ON PINTEREST
pinterest.com/chipbellauthor
/the-jake-sullivan-series

**TAKE THE TIME TO REVIEW
THIS BOOK ON AMAZON**
amazon.com/author
/chipbellauthor.com

Made in the USA
Middletown, DE
01 December 2023

44140364R00159